Living Legacy

Among the Dead

By
R.W.K. Clark

Published in the United States by Clarkltd.
Po Box 45313 Rio Rancho, NM 87174
info@clarkltd.com

Edition 1

United States Copyright Office
TX8-278-942 May 2016

Library of Congress Control Number
LCCN: 2017907099

International Standard Book Numbers
ISBN-13: 978-0692517246 (paperback)
ISBN-13: 978-1948312196 (paperback)
ISBN-13: 978-1948312202 (hardcover)
ASIN: B014HW9XZO (Kindle)

/200801

CONTENTS

PRAISES FOR LIVING LEGACY

"I would recommend it to zombie lovers everywhere.... just bring your own bottled water."
— *Fiction Author Rhoda D'Ettore on Amazon*

"Definitely one of the best zombie-themed books I have read this year."
— *LJ on Amazon*

"I really enjoyed the uniqueness of this story and was captivated until the end."
— *Sonal on Amazon*

"The plot is super interesting and if you're a fan of crisis related stories, you'd fall in love."
— *Kalpana Kucheria on Amazon*

"Love, thrills, suspense, heartbreak, and zombies."
— *Bryleebaker on barnesandnoble*

"A burgeoning romance and a zombie apocalypse, what more could you want in a book."
— *Brynsgreen on barnesandnoble*

"A tale of zombies, fear, and love that I found myself turning page after page."
— *Amazon Customer*

"An unusual concept that works brilliantly. Very

well written with plenty of action and very hard to put down."
— *Michael Naylor on Amazon*

"Another wonderful book by Mr. Clark that will have his readers thirsty (no pun intended)"
— *Julie on Amazon*

"Suspense, action, and a quick paced writing style that keeps you moving from page to page with an eager hunger for what comes next."
— *Dawn Dolly Golden on Amazon*

"One of the coolest stories that I've read in a long time."
— *Sherrill R. Lewis on Amazon*

"This isn't your typical zombie apocalypse novel."
— *Andrew on Amazon*

"Strongly recommend this awesome supernatural, zombie, sci-fi romance!"
— *K. R. Shaw on Amazon*

"Unique and compelling storyline grabbed my attention."
— *Cadenroberts on barnesandnoble*

ACKNOWLEDGMENTS

I dedicate this novel to my wonderful readers and for all the amazing people I've met and those I haven't. To my family and loved ones, all your support will not be forgotten.

This book was made possible by reviews from readers like you.

Thank you

R.W.K. Clark

PROLOGUE

Jim Richardson thrust his hand into his pocket and withdrew a grimy handkerchief. It had once been white, but after years and years of soaking up the sweat from his brow, it had turned a faded brownish-yellow that even the strongest bleach could not remedy. He looked it over, smiled to himself, and mopped his forehead with a single swipe. As he buried the piece of cloth back into his pocket he looked over his 'office': a large space filled with chemical vats and meters, alarms and tubes, all of which either brought in the materials needed to make plastic or brought in what was needed to break it down. It didn't matter which; the vats contained the volatile substances because no other holder could.

Jim had worked for All-Purpose Plastics for thirty years, and he was beginning to count the years and days until his retirement. He dreamed about that moment in time when fishing and beer were the priority. He had no college degree; he was only aware of the dangers of his job because they told him. They had needed someone they could trust to follow strict protocol at all times, and he had proven himself trustworthy. They liked him, and they always made sure his bread was abundantly buttered. He made great money, and even though he didn't get a regular vacation period (or even a day off, for that matter), they gave him a brand new car to drive every year, paid his mortgage off in full. They generously allowed his wife to remodel their home, footing the bill to stop her nagging about his hours. He loved the hours, truth be told. It protected him from her nagging as well.

Today had been a bit off from the beginning: Jim had risen at four, showered, and made it to the plant about a quarter to five. Things had gone smoothly until exactly 7:23 a.m., nearly two-and-a-half hours later. While walking his rounds in his tank, he had noticed a leak. The substance leaking was toxic; he knew this because they told him, and he believed every word they said. It had formed a substantial puddle on the floor, where a film had begun to form over the top as the hot goop cooled. According to the procedure he had to gear up in a yellow rubber jumpsuit and clean it up immediately. There was a special tank in one area of his worksite where he would dispose of the substance. It was filled with water and would not only supposedly neutralize the substance, but it would also subsequently dispose of it. It would be carried out of the building to its new home, wherever that was. To a facility on the outskirts of town, he believed. He believed this because they had told him so, and they never lied.

There was the equivalent of three large scoop shovels of goop to eradicate, and at one point he paid close attention to the stuff in his shovel. It had a weird color and appearance. When the light reflected off it, one could swear the stuff was... moving.

He shoved the thought from his mind and continued to do his job. He put a special container under the leak, and with awkwardly gloved hands shut off connecting valves and repaired the damaged piping. In no time the equipment and the entire area itself was secure. He was up and safely running again. He filled out a three-page report, which was the worst part of his job. Jim personally walked it, in duplicate, to the office of the scientist in charge of this particular project and the Big Cheese himself.

Turning the paperwork in was generally uneventful, aside from a few questions to make sure he had followed procedures. He had, to a tee. He took great pride in being thorough and trustworthy; they were his best characteristics, according to the powers that be. He put in the rest of the day's hours with nothing changing, except that he walked the floor for inspection rounds a few more times than usual. Accidents had a way of making you gun-shy for a bit.

∞

The next day was the same as the last, the same as always. Get up, go to work, do your work, go home. But today Jim had a severe bout of heartburn, so severe that nothing seemed to remedy it. He noticed a rash on his right wrist and forearm which was bothersome as well. He applied calamine lotion from the tank's first aid kit, but it did little to help the itching at all, and he was thirsty, wow was he thirsty! He chugged down more water that day alone than he had over the last five days combined, he was quite sure. Maybe he was coming down with a bug.

By the following Monday, Jim Richardson was in a bad way. Not only had his skin taken on a grayish pallor, but it was also sort of numb. His thirst increased steadily, and while his heartburn had ceased, he had not eaten a bite of food in nearly five full days. He just didn't feel like anything sounded good. He was tired, but not worn out, and strangely enough, he felt strong and energetic, staying at work for the last two nights because he just couldn't sleep. He noticed a lack of interest in everything, even his work. His wife expressed concern which he blew off clearly to her face. She nagged until he put a hole through the front door and went to work, where he had stayed. Okay, so he never had a temper problem, but why did she have to be such a nag?

Now he felt a slight tug of concern. Not for his own personal well-being; he was sure he was fine. He was concerned that maybe the spill had caused a problem for him, therefore causing a problem for All-Purpose Plastics. That was the last thing he wanted. His life sort of revolved around this place, after all.

He filled his thermos with water from the tap, and slamming it down in record time, he headed to the lab to talk to Sandberg, the head scientist in charge of the project. When he reached the main lab, he cracked the glass door about four inches.

"Sandberg, are you in here? It's Jim." There was no immediate response, but Jim went in anyway. If Mike Sandberg wasn't in here, he would just have a seat. He would be back soon enough.

There were three chrome and plastic chairs next to the glass door. There was a cheap plastic coffee table with two copies of *Newsday* thrown carelessly on top. It was all covered in a layer of gray dust. He sat, the air escaping him loudly, and looked around the main lab entry area.

To his right was a large green metal desk with a rubber top. A blotter calendar with the year 1998 was on top, and next to that an old-style cradle phone with five white buttons and one red one sat lifeless. A coffee cup with upside-down pencils sat opposite the phone; not one of them had its lead intact.

To his left were two heavy wood institutional-type doors. One led to the actual lab; its window was covered with a magazine cover from the other side. The other door led to Sandberg's office. Its window was not covered, and the light was on.

Jim stood and walked the fifteen feet to Sandberg's door. He stumbled twice but managed to keep his footing. What was that about? Ah, dang, keep your balance, Jim. He tried to smile to himself, but his face did not cooperate. He wasn't surprised and didn't care.

After three short raps on Mike's door, the knob turned, and there stood Sandberg. Jim hadn't seen him since turning in his report on last week's incident, and the look on Mike's face told Jim that the scientist didn't like what he saw.

"Jim, what the heck happened to you?" Sandberg was so shocked by Jim's appearance he couldn't even close his mouth. His eyes got wider as Jim got closer. "Sit down, man, you look like death warmed over!"

"I was hoping you could tell me, Mike. Since we work with such delicate and secretive garbage, I thought I'd better come to you before seeing my HMO." His voice was no more than a croak. It took Mike a minute to piece his sounds into a sentence he could comprehend. Jim sat in a chair to the right of Mike's desk and looked up at him expectantly.

"I'm glad you did that, Jim. Tell me all that is going on with you. When did it start? I'm sorry if I look a bit overwhelmed, but have you looked in the mirror lately?" Jim thought about that, or, at least, he tried. He couldn't recall the last time he had looked in a mirror at all. Jim typically showered in the morning before leaving the house, but he had been here forever, it seemed. The house… what house? He found himself confused about where his home was or what it even looked like.

"I don't know, Mike." He must have even looked confused, which seemed to startle the scientist. Mike walked around his desk and fished a small round shaving mirror from the bottom right-hand drawer. He brought it to Jim and held it up to his face.

His eyes were dead, just dead. There was no color to the irises; they seemed as black as the pupils themselves. His skin was not just dark gray. There were patches which appeared papery; they were even beginning to peel at the edges. The left nostril of his nose looked like it was deteriorating or something, and his tongue was black on the surface as well.

"What the…?" Jim felt a bit of emotional discomfort at the sight, but at the same time, he felt a smug satisfaction that he didn't comprehend at all. He decided to go with it.

Mike asked again for Jim to tell him everything. Richardson did the best he could. His voice was almost nonexistent, and he felt like he was almost in a trance. The funny thing was, the more he heard Mike's voice, the more annoyed and angry he became. It was akin to sandpaper on his skin.

Mike went around his desk and picked up his phone. "I'm calling Mikelson." Mikelson was the president of All-Purpose and the only other person Jim came into close contact with. "What was the first sign that you recognized that told you things were… off?"

"It seemed like I looked pale, and I had a rash. Can I have a drink of water?" Mike went to a small sink in the corner and, fetching a Styrofoam cup from the cupboard over the sink, he brought it to Jim.

It was gone in seconds. Jim lurched blindly to the sink and managed to down five more before leaning contentedly against the basin and looking back at Sandberg. Something was sparking in Sandberg's mind. Something bad.

He recalled the preliminary testing which had been done on the substance Jim was in charge of overseeing. Testing such as this was extensive; so extensive that this particular battery of tests had lasted more than two years. You find a problem, you rectify it, and you move on. They had had plenty of rounds of this cycle. The plastic was called 'Soligel,' and it promised to be the plastic of the future if they could just iron out the bugs.

The first handful of problems were simple, easily rectifiable. Small things, like chemical imbalances in the 'recipe.' The real problem had reared its ugly head when it came to testing for safety around humans and animals. None of the team had any problems, but the experimental animals had an issue. They seemed to almost die, yet they were living. Dissection experiments had shown no organs were functioning in the rats except for their brains. They were dusty death from the inside out. They had been unable to pinpoint the cause, and lack of further evidence of destruction had led them to virtually cover up the entire shortcoming.

Now it seemed they had acted too soon.

Harvey Mikelson answered his emergency extension, and Sandberg used code to fill him in. He didn't want to alarm Jim, who now had his head down and was drinking directly from the faucet. This was bad indeed. Mikelson told Mike he would be to his office shortly to help assess the situation and make a decision regarding the proper course of action. They were making millions off Soligel. If they pulled the product now, well, let's just say crap rolls downhill.

Sandberg recalled how the rats that had not undergone dissection seemed to change behaviorally before their very eyes. If they were eating and one rat began to nibble on the kibble in another's dish, things became violent. One such confrontation between the rodents ended when each limb was pulled off another; he lay squirming in his own dust. Mike had to remove the animal's head before it would stop moving. This led to another round of… well, playing, really. They would pick the most violent rats with the shaggiest fur and the deadest eyes. The rats were then subjected to various means of torture, just to see how long it would take for them to die. In the end, they concluded brain death was the only way, by any means possible.

Because they had abandoned their studies to move on with the actual production of Soligel, they really didn't know what had spawned the adverse reaction the rats had to the substance. Frankly, none of them had cared. The money began rolling in before they had even put a pen to any contracts. They had gone blind, with greed.

There was a sharp knock at Sandberg's office door, and Mikelson made his way in just as Mike had convinced the staggering Richardson to take a seat again. Jim didn't even notice that the chair had been moved; it was much closer to the sink.

"Jim. I hear you aren't feeling well." Harvey Mikelson's voice was deep, and a bit gravelly, matching his imposing six-foot-four build to a tee. "Tell me what has been going on."

Now Jim found he was really feeling pissed. Repetition. Why all the repetition? He opened his mouth and made the words, but the sound of his voice was monstrous. It gurgled and smacked of his own rotten saliva.

Harvey listened as best he could, pretending to putt with a golf club he had brought in with him. "Mm-hmm," he would mutter in an appeasing fashion whenever Jim seemed to pause.

"I'm tired, so tired," he croaked to Mikelson.

"What you need is rest, a long rest," said Harvey. Mikelson was right. Jim believed him because Harvey would never lie to him.

Jim Richardson didn't even hear the swooshing of the wind as Mikelson's golf club swung hard through the air, and thanks to the poisonous toxins in his body he didn't feel a thing when the sturdy club connected with his rotting skull, ripping the skin of his neck and disconnecting his head completely from his body.

It landed in the sink, drops of water landing in his gaping mouth.

Harvey Mikelson looked at Sandberg with a grim smile and said, "Fore…!"

CHAPTER 1

It's Thursday night.

As I lie in my bed in my UCLA dorm room, the fog begins to clear from my mind. I was sleeping. I was suddenly aware that I was sleeping no longer. What woke me? I listened closely to the sounds around me; the room was too dark to see. I was soon able to identify the sound of my roommate, Lilith, moving around. As I strained to hear what she was doing I realized she had returned to the sink; she was having a drink of water… again. I groaned and tossed off my light blankets, swinging my feet to the floor. The floor felt ice-cold, even though the night was comfortable, warm enough for the windows to be open.

"Lil, are you awake? Are you thirsty again? Maybe you're sick. You should see the campus medical." All I could hear in response was her gulping down the chilled tap liquid. I looked at the clock: 11:30 p.m. I had turned in around 8:30 p.m., early for me, due to an important biology exam. I was prepared, but I wanted to be well-rested. This was the second time Lilith had managed to wake me attempting to quench her nagging thirst.

As I listened to the sounds she made while drinking

I felt a pang of jealousy; I found the water to be repulsive. It began with a slightly bitter taste which put me off, and it had grown exceedingly worse over the last few months. I simply couldn't stomach it, couldn't get it past the nose on my face, but it seemed to bother no one else. I was dying to taste good water, to feel it run its course from my mouth to my stomach, but I couldn't. The fact was that everyone else continued to drink it heartily, even in its putrid state. Now it was flashing all over television that we were actually short of water all over. They said nothing regarding the smell and rank flavor. None of this made any sense to me, but not another soul seemed to bat an eye at the situation.

The water wasn't the only issue, and neither was the blasé attitude everyone else had toward it. These were just the tip of the iceberg. The truth of the matter is that these things were accompanied by a problem which brought a cold chill of fear and apprehension to me: no one was the same. At that point I could not quite put a finger on the differences I saw, so subtle they were. But they were there nonetheless. Everyone was just... off. At that point, it felt much like it must feel to awaken in a parallel universe where everything is the same, but it is darkly different. This is the only way I can describe the changes in personality I was witnessing at that time. Now I know it to be about so much more.

My entire life had begun to be characterized by apprehension and suspicion when it came to everyone I came in contact with, on campus and off. In those initial days, before I knew what was happening to the world around me, I simply thought I was, slowly but surely losing my mind. How could everyone be different except me? I had started to conclude that I was not only paranoid but sported fanciful illusions as well. As I became aware that the opposite was true, I felt an odd mixture of terror and relief that was quite disconcerting.

People were changing, and not just in Los Angeles. They were changing all over the world. Initially, it was just behavioral: shorter fuses, longer periods with less sleep, etc. Soon I began to notice the paling of everyone's skin. There was an emptiness in their eyes which actually seemed to progress, and I can honestly say that was the worst part then. The look, or lack thereof, in their eyes. No one was home upstairs but me.

The bathroom light came on, illuminating the room to the point that I could actually take things in. I stood to use the toilet and Lilith came out of the bathroom at the same time.

"Did I wake you again?" Her voice had no inflection; the statement didn't even sound like a question. It was a dead sentence that fell limp and lifeless from her mouth.

"I had to pee anyway," I replied. "No big deal. How are you feeling?"

"Fine. Great." That was her only response as she got into her bed and covered herself with what appeared to be at least three blankets, the top of which was a heavy quilted comforter. How could she possibly be cold? It had to be eighty degrees outside, and there was no breeze. This was another out-of-sorts behavior which I had taken note of recently, and not just with Lilith; most students and professors were donning sweaters and jackets most all the time, and it was September.

"Have you thought about seeing the doctor at all?" Lilith emitted an angry growl; she had begun to sleep, and my words had roused her. Like I said, short fuses.

I relieved myself and returned to the comfort of my bed, but sleep would elude me for the remainder of the night. I tossed and turned incessantly, thinking about Lilith, the water, and the way the world around me seemed to be spinning out of control. I was losing my mind…

I wound up turning on the small desk lamp next to me on my nightstand and pulling my biology studies into the bed with me. I figured if the light didn't bother Lilith I could drill my notes even deeper into my brain. After a night with no sleep, I would need all the help I could get. Thankfully my roomie didn't even twitch; she slept like the dead until around 1:15 a.m. At that point, she rose to have more water, and this pattern continued until 7:30 a.m. that morning, when I went to seek out nourishment in the dining hall.

The day would present more tests than just the one I faced in Biology.

CHAPTER 2

While this day remains somewhat of a blur in my mind, it is also painfully clear. This would be the day things became so much clearer to me. It would be the day that would prove to change my entire life. I would figure things out: I would see them for what they really were.

After having a small breakfast, I crossed campus and took my Biology exam, feeling quite confident that I had aced it. This was a relief, as I had been worried about the lack of sleep I had gotten. I left the lab almost walking on air and experiencing a second wind. The test had taken three hours; it would soon be time for lunch. I decided to stroll to the business district and find a nice coffee and a sandwich.

The walk was refreshing and beautiful, aesthetically anyway. Everyone I looked at seemed to lurch along forcefully, their gait entirely off. They were all pale and lacked energy, but yet they strove to tackle their next task, whatever that might be. Every individual I came across, even at the café, was detached, giving short answers to questions or asking questions consisting of few words. There were no conversations or laughter;

there was a dark cloud over the entire world.

While having my lunch I noticed something which was not only disturbing, it brought chills to my flesh. Either I had failed to notice it before, or it was a new change taking place in those around me. Areas of the pale skin on these people were actually turning a greenish-gray, and I noticed that on several individuals (my waiter included) these gray patches appeared to be flaking or peeling away. The guy who served me was actually leaving traces of himself behind, and this compelled me to pay closer attention to everyone else. The metamorphosis was obviously reaching another stage. The entire café was guzzling water uncontrollably.

It was at this point that I finally determined to take some of the tap water from my bathroom sink and put it under the microscope at the lab. This was simply out of control, and no one seemed the least bit concerned but me! What had taken me so long to come to this decision I could not say, but once I got the idea in my head, I couldn't let it go. My stomach had grown sick at the sight of my waiter's deteriorating flesh, so I paid my bill and left the remainder of my Reuben and fries on the table next to my coffee and the full glass of putrid water they had brought me.

The Biology department was fully stocked with anything I could possibly need to collect the water without contaminating it myself, so on the way home I stopped and obtained several sterile collection kits to hold my samples. I used one to get water from the ladies' room in that building. I then made my way back to the dorm and collected a sample from my bathroom. I also grabbed my purple backpack with my books and cleaned it out, with the exception of a new spiral notebook and my laptop and cell phone. I also made sure to have a highlighter, pencil, and pen. Then I packed my two water samples and the rest of my collection kits inside as well and made my way back to the business district. I had three kits left, and I planned to collect water samples at a couple of businesses in town, and I would also hike to the Los Angeles River and acquire a sample from there.

Other than a few growls and shady glances from those I had begun to mentally refer to as zombies, my venture was uneventful. During my excursion, I made it a point to pay close attention to those around me, and I noticed that cars on the street seemed to veer quite often; this alarmed me. These people were struggling to walk properly, yet they were operating motor vehicles? The true impact of the situation was sinking in, and my concern was gradually giving way to fear.

I also took notice of a number of disagreements between random people on the street. Dead, lifeless voices were reaching heated tones, and this was taking place everywhere I seemed to go. I made it a point to keep to myself; I was scared to death, and the worst was yet to come.

With my final sample in hand, I headed back to campus and the Biology lab to make use of the equipment there. I planned to take thorough notes and then hit the library with my findings so I could sort this mess out as best I could. The nagging sickness I felt in my gut was tugging at my brain, and I was determined to calm it with something other than liquor, though that solution had crossed my mind more than once.

I grabbed a bus that was headed to the campus and found a seat in the rear near the back door; I wanted to get off and begin my testing with as little hindrance as possible. The campus was a good fifteen-minute ride, so I wrapped my arms around my backpack, which sat securely on my lap, and settled in for the ride. It was at this point that one of the gray-faces who had gotten on the bus with me attempted to take a seat next to an older woman. The woman was staring blankly out the window when the guy sat, but as the bus pulled away from the curb and gained speed she turned to the man and asked, "Could you sit somewhere else?" Once again, the voice coming from her mouth was flat and lifeless, but she looked a bit annoyed by his presence. It was the most emotion I had witnessed from anyone in what seemed like a very long time.

"You sit somewhere else," was his response.

Suddenly, the woman swung on him with a mighty backhand. The strike connected fully with the front of his face, knocking him out of the seat and flaying the flesh from his nose as though it were nothing but butter. A growl came from deep within him, and he appeared to feel no pain as he stood and went at her. My heart was pounding, and I could feel the boiling hot blood pumping through my veins. He grabbed her and lifted her from her seat, throwing her like rags to the floor of the bus. It was then that things became nightmarish, horrible, to say the least. As she lay there struggling against her weight to rise to her feet the man knelt over her and took a hearty bite from her cheek. She gurgled and snarled, but did not scream; no, I was the one doing the screaming, but no one paid attention to me. They were all looking on with slight half-smiles and saliva-covered lips. The man feasted on his squirming meal until the fight became too much for him, at which point he punched effortlessly through her chest, easing her fight to nearly nothing.

The bus pulled over to let off a passenger in the front, and I didn't hesitate: I ran for dear life, off the bus and in the direction of the campus. I know I was sobbing uncontrollably, and I do believe I screamed much of the way back. In retrospect, however, I believe my screaming was in my head, but to me, it was deafening.

R.W.K. Clark

CHAPTER 3

I ran all the way to the dorms, my fear driving me to bypass the lab completely. I ran into my room and slammed the door, making sure it was closed tight and locked securely. I then flung my backpack to the floor and fell to my bed sobbing hysterically and in a state of hyperventilation.

"Get control, get control," I repeated to myself over and over. My body was shaking uncontrollably, and I felt nothing but ice cold, despite the thin layer of sweat covering my body. Every noise I heard on the other side of my dorm room door was one of them; it could be no one else. I was the only real human I knew.

"Come on, Alicia; get control of yourself." I forced myself to control my breathing, keeping my eyes glued to the door until I was calm enough to think clearly. I had to get to the lab; I had to figure out what was going on. Either the world had gone mad, or I was dreaming. My mind flashed back to the violent scene on the bus, and my stomach gave a violent lurch. I barely made it to the bathroom before the vomit came, and I retched until nothing more would come. I could not even rinse the taste from my mouth because the water was poisoned. I made my way to the mini-fridge Lilith, and I shared and fished a soda from it. I swished it around in my mouth and spat in the bathroom sink. I then guzzled about half of it. I was dying of thirst.

In an effort to clear my mind more quickly and keep in touch with reality I began to vigorously pace the room, sorting my thoughts as I went. I kept a constant eye on the door, and I listened closely to any sounds coming from the other side. I heard many pass, but no one slowed or stopped.

∞

After around an hour, I was relaxed enough to talk myself into continuing on with my mission.

I grabbed my backpack, which held my precious water samples, and cracked the door to my room open just enough to scope out the hallway. One girl loped toward a door at the end of the hall; she had her back to me and didn't seem to be aware that I was watching her. I took advantage of the opportunity and, making sure I had my room key, I entered the hall, tugging the locked door firmly shut behind me.

The walk to the lab was uneventful, and I was panic-stricken and highly cautious. I noticed that even though everyone seemed to be in this monstrous state, most took absolutely no notice of me or of each other. What could have sparked the violent scene on the bus? Certainly, something very specific motivated the woman's dreadful mood swing, which had started the entire nightmare. What was really going on?

Once I reached the lab, I took to the isolated workstation in the far corner so I could be left to my testing. I gathered the things I would need and began the process of testing all the samples I had acquired that day. I took vigorous notes, and I found myself scrawling thoughts and theories more than I would have liked. My initial findings, though completely mind-boggling and unrecognizable to me, were petrifying. I had detected a bacterium in the water, and though I didn't recognize it from any resource books in the lab, I knew I would be able to identify it at the library. At least, I could if it had ever been recognized before.

The bacterium was in each and every sample, and it was rampantly abundant. The worst part was that it seemed to have attached itself to what I considered unidentifiable molecules within the water, and the bacteria were growing at an alarmingly rapid pace. How I wished I had a pure, clean sample to compare them to, but alas, I did not. I needed to conduct as much research as possible to identify the unknown molecules and bacteria; I had a feeling that the turn the world had taken was due to the water, and could be attributed to nothing else. I needed to solve this mystery and find a way to rectify the situation and the lives of everyone around me. As I packed my things into my backpack, I vowed to myself that I would ingest no water at any time. It wouldn't be difficult, the very smell turned my stomach. I would have to learn to get by without clean water.

As for bathing, I had a microwave in the room

which I used for minor cooking tasks. I figured that the next day I would boil some water in it and check it out in the lab after it had cleared out in the afternoon. If boiling worked to clean it up, I would sponge-bathe until the world straightened out… or not. Otherwise, I would resort to getting some dry shampoo and baby wipes at the drug store. Something had to be done because to smell myself on top of all this chaos was an unbearable thought.

I left the lab, backpack slung over one shoulder, and I headed for the library to do some research regarding my findings. I made my way with my eyes to the ground, keeping my pace up. I hoped I could figure out the problem, and the solution, as soon as possible.

CHAPTER 4

As I approached the library, it was nearing 5:00 p.m., and I took note of all the zombies loitering around the front entrance outside. Mostly they were shuffling around and staring blankly. One kid, about 20 years old, was struggling to operate his bicycle properly. I was filled with an overwhelming sense of trepidation at the thought of coming anywhere near him, but I bucked myself up, and stared straight ahead, I began to pass him. Just as I got by him his frustrations overwhelmed him; he simply could not put the peddling and maneuvering of his bike together. He lifted the bicycle over his head and violently smashed it to the ground, loud screams and growls emitting from his lips. He bent over and retrieved the bike and repeated his actions. I began to shake, backing away from him fearfully as he did this a number of times. The others looked on, and it seemed with each repetition of his actions they became more and more riled up, even enjoying the violence he exhibited. I finally got my wits about me, and even as the group of gray-faces came closer, I was able to snap out of my petrified trance and make a break for the library door. I hoped the group out front meant the building was empty.

There were three people inside. Two wandered aimlessly to the rear of the common area, while the third sat intently reading a book and taking notes. He seemed a bit different, as if he had a purpose, knew what he wanted to do, and was able to effectively get the job done. This was not characteristic of the questionably warm-blooded people who now inhabit the world. In an effort to get a better view I sat only about three chairs from him, and while I took my sample test notes out of my backpack, I kept one eye on him.

His face was full of color; he was pretty hot, actually. There was no gray tint to his tone. His eyes had life in them. I cleared my throat without being too obvious, and his head snapped up quickly. We made eye contact immediately.

"This is a library, you know. You should be a bit more still." His words seemed confrontational, but his eyes were smiling. Did he see that I wasn't a zombie? I could tell he wasn't; maybe the appearance of my normalcy was obvious to him as well.

"I know... frog in my throat." I couldn't help but smile fully at him. I was so relieved to see a normal human being that I was literally on the verge of tears. I held back with all my might. "I'm Alicia... uh, Alicia Gaden."

I half-expected him to jump up and begin shuffling and groaning, as though I had jumped to dangerous conclusions. I was quickly learning that, while the zombies were fairly functional, they seemed to irritate quickly, and their ability to control their irritation was minimal. Had I really just set off another gray-face?

"I'm Jace Booth. You look flushed. In this day and age that is an awesome thing to see. Normal?"

I released the breath I had been holding with full force; I'm sure it was audible, but I didn't care. "Yes. Absolutely. You are a sight for sore eyes!"

Jace laid his pen on top of his notebook and sat back, crossing his arms over his chest. "What would possess a normal young lady like yourself to brave the deathly troops to come and study?"

Young lady? I was 21, and he couldn't be much older than I, if at all. He was gentlemanly. "I'm doing a bit of research. I'm a Biology major, and…"

"Biology, huh? I'm majoring in Chemistry myself. What brings you to the library with all this chaos? You must have more balls than any girl I've ever met. Things are looking worse for the world than ever before, yet here you are."

I opened my mouth to respond, but just then a commotion started toward the rear of the common area. A commotion between the two zombies. Jace turned in his chair when he caught wind of the grunts and growls emitting from the rear of the room. I just stared.

One zombie was holding a large book; the other wanted the book. It was that simple. What began as a two-second tug-of-war soon turned into a full-fledged battle, only it wasn't fists that began to fly. It was teeth gnashing and hands tearing at flesh. I could not bear yet another gray-face confrontation, and within seconds I dropped to the floor and situated myself under the study table for sanctuary. Jace joined me seconds later. I welcomed his company wholeheartedly.

He began with, "Hi!" Then he continued by putting my feelings into words for me: "I don't think my stomach can take another match of monsters chowing down on each other. It seems like it's happening more and more often lately."

"Wow, so it's not just me…"

"No. It's reality." This was his only reply. We turned our attention to listening to the wet chewing and crunching noises coming from the common's rear. I plugged my ears and clenched my eyes tightly shut. I don't know how long I stayed that way, but when I opened my eyes, Jace was staring at the floor. He sat on his rear with his knees bent, and his arms were wrapped tightly around his legs. I took my fingers from my ears, catching his attention.

"Don't worry. I think it's almost over."

The only thing I could hear was a bit of grunting and a few wet sounds, but the noises had greatly diminished. After a few moments, I heard shuffling, awkward steps. The door to the library opened and closed, and all was silent.

Jace peered over the edge of the study desk and scanned the area before saying, "I think it's over. We should be okay to come out."

Slowly we emerged from the safety we had found. The library was quiet, and there was no movement anywhere. Jace looked me over, and I him. "So, what are you doing here? It doesn't make much sense for either of us. I mean, do we really expect to finish our college educations at this point?" He gave a weak chuckle. "I'm just trying to keep my mind on anything sane. My studies are all I can find."

"I'm trying to figure out what is going on here," I replied.

His eyes widened. "Really? What are you doing, exactly?"

I took a deep breath, and casting one final look around the library, plopped into my chair. "I'm pretty sure it's the water. I mean, the water is repulsive to me, but it seems we see these freaks slurping it down every chance they get. I don't drink it or wash with it, and I'm still okay. Are you drinking it?"

"Ah, the common denominator!" Jace grabbed his things and moved to the chair across from mine. "I can't drink it. Wouldn't want to if I tried. I'm living on a diet of bottled pop and gallons of the distilled stuff from the store." Now there was a solution. Why hadn't I thought of that? "So, have you done any research or come up with any ideas?"

I swallowed the massive lump in my throat and put my hands beneath my thighs to steady their obvious tremor. "Actually, I gathered several water samples from a few different places, including the Los Angeles River, and I took them to the Bio lab and ran some tests. While I can't specify what I found, I did find some pretty unsettling things. I came to the library to research my findings."

"So, do you wanna tell me what you do know specifically? I mean, maybe I can help with research. That's what I've been doing. I have no real idea what's going on, so I have been trying to track down any historical circumstance which could give me answers. I must say, there are none, and I would like to narrow things down before I become the main course myself." Jace smiled grimly, which prompted me to do the same.

"Well, what I found from my samples was an obvious bacterium, and it was attached to unknown molecules in each sample I tested. Had I had the materials I needed while I was at the lab I would have been able to identify the molecules; they looked fairly basic and generally harmless to me. But these bacteria were reproducing at a high rate of speed, and it appeared very volatile. In one sample it was obviously destroying all of the life it came in contact with. From what I saw, I can only conclude that not one of the people walking around us, eating and beating each other, is truly alive. I'm convinced they are dead… zombies." I inhaled sharply and tore my eyes from his confused, overwhelmed face, settling them on a spot on the floor.

"Alicia, are you serious? Do you have any idea what you found?" He looked completely incredulous, but I could tell him nothing but what I had learned. I reached for my notebook and motioned for him to sit in the chair next to mine. He came around the desk and sat as I opened the spiral. I had both sketched and written out my observations, and I proceeded to break it all down for him. He listened intently to everything I had to say, and when I was finished, he looked me in the eye.

"Do you watch any television? Have you heard anything about the water on the news?"

I shook my head. "I don't. I heard on the radio several times that the world is experiencing an urgent water shortage, but I didn't take it to heart until today. I mean, is it a shortage, or are these monsters trying to keep it all for themselves? They appear to be seriously addicted to it."

He thought for a moment. "Do you think the wi-fi here is active? We could go to search and see if we can find any news releases that relate."

This was a brilliant idea, one I more than welcomed. We gathered our things and made our way to the second floor cautiously. It was empty. Not a soul was there. We went to a table that gave us a full sight of the staircase, and I opened my bag and freed my laptop from its confines. In no time we were online, and we were about to learn more than we ever thought we could or would.

R.W.K. Clark

CHAPTER 5

Jace and I got settled into our new spot and got my laptop booted up and online. I really wasn't sure where to begin, so I simply searched the term "tap water" for starters. It was a stretch, but maybe I could find something, anything, that would lead us to the next step. Of course, as far as I knew, Jace and I were the only ones left unaffected by the recent situation. Maybe someone else out there was randomly attempting to share information in hopes of learning something as well.

We scrolled through the options which were available for us. The first thing I found which appeared even remotely related to our situation was a video of a newscast which discussed prescription drugs in the tap water virtually everywhere. The video was just a couple of minutes long, but it was very informative, and it set my mind off to the races with ideas.

When it ended, I turned to Jace and stated, "I want to find a book which can give me some examples of the molecular structure of various pharmaceuticals."

He gave me a smile. "I know just the book you are looking for. Wait here." He jumped up and disappeared, but I could hear him just a few stacks away. When he returned he toted a massive volume entitled *Molecular Biopharmaceutics*. My eyes lit up as I reached out to take the volume from his hands.

"Perfect!" I exclaimed. "Just what I'm looking for." I reached for my spiral notebook. I had sketched numerous things I had found in the water samples, the normal yet unidentified molecules I had pinpointed. For the next couple of hours, we paged through the resource book and made comparisons, even identifying many of them. We finally reached a pretty solid conclusion. Just as the news bit had said, the tap water was virtually filled with pharmaceutical drugs and a massive variety at that.

∞

It was now 10:00 p.m., and while I kept expecting to be kicked out of the library, my mind was fully aware this was likely not going to happen. That didn't stop both of us from keeping one eye on the door at all times and glancing nervously over our shoulders. We even spoke in hushed tones, even though we knew we were alone in the building.

I noted the name of each drug next to the drawing I had created, making for easy identification while we continued to investigate. The next step was to identify the bacteria which appeared to have adhered themselves to the drug molecules in the water. It was my turn to fetch a book from the stacks.

Jace accompanied me on my search, adamant that I

not be alone, regardless of the fact that we were obviously under no threat. I think both of us knew that we were better safe than sorry. Together we made our way to the stack of choice, and I ran my finger along the spines until I located the volume I was looking for, *The Bacteria: Their Origin, Structure, Function, and Antibiosis: First Edition*. To the best of my ability, I had sketched the bacterium, though it hadn't been easy. In my studies, I had never seen one quite so complex or aggressive, but I was sure the mental picture of it in my mind was burned into it forever. It was a monstrosity, and very aggressive.

∞

By nearly midnight we were three-quarters of the way through the book, with no results. The closest we came was a rare bacterium originating in Zimbabwe which had proven to eat individuals from the inside out. Recorded cases always resulted in death, but not walking death, and from what we read it had been completely contained years ago. By 1:00 a.m. we had exhausted our search through the volume to no avail.

"I'm going to go out on a limb here," I began. "The bacteria I found in the samples closely resembled the flesh eater here." I had dog-eared the page previously, and now I flipped back to it to expand on my idea. "My theory is that the bacterium I saw is somehow related, or perhaps even a mutated version. We can ask ourselves how, and that would help us figure out what steps to take to turn this thing around."

Jace's face went grim. "Alicia, if these individuals are really roaming around dead, and functioning at the same time, I don't see a way to reverse anything. I'm guessing we can only figure out how to clean the water and go on from here."

I went into thought for a moment. "Let's say you are right. If that's the case, then it is vital that we take steps to clean the water. Maybe without it, these zombie creeps will eventually die for real. I just know that we can't live without drinking water, and baby wipes and dry hair shampoo aren't going to keep me clean forever."

We began to discuss our idea. The news clip about the pharmaceuticals in the water had clearly stated that modern-day filtration systems are simply not designed to eliminate the trace metals and drugs in the water supply. We needed to figure out the best method to do just that. The question was: were we going to do it for survival alone, or as an eradication attempt as well?

My eyes were getting scratchy, and my back and neck ached. Jace was frequently stretching or pacing, giving away his discomfort level. I suggested we call it a night, but he did not want to separate.

"Your own dorm mate is in this state. I won't let you go to your room and take any risks. Look, I'm perfectly harmless, really." He smiled. "You are welcome to come to my apartment. It's about six blocks from campus. Or, if you prefer, we can stay here and catch a few zees behind the main desk. My only issue with that is the zombie librarian will be here at six in the morning. Who knows how far this thing has progressed in the last several hours?"

We finally settled on the janitor's closet. We barricaded the door with chairs from the library and, settling our heads on our backpacks, snuggled slightly for a bit of warmth. As we lay next to each other, we talked about our tentative plans for the following day, finally drifting off to a restless sleep.

R.W.K. Clark

CHAPTER 6

My eyes fluttered open to see Jace quietly moving chairs from in front of the closet door. I sat up and rubbed my eyes, then continued watching him. He turned to place a chair out of the way and, noticing me sitting there, said a gentle 'good morning.' I smiled and reciprocated the waking greeting.

We gathered our bags and Jace took me by the hand. He opened the door and looked around, making sure we had a clear, safe exit. The first thing he did was steer me into a chair at a study desk. "Take out a book or something. Look as normal as possible." He sat across from me and dug through his bag, pulling out a notebook and pen.

I looked around the room. There were four gray-faces present. They appeared to be wandering aimlessly, with absolutely no purpose. Jace waved his hand in front of my face, snapping me back to reality.

"I did a lot of thinking last night, and here are some ideas. One, I turned over the temper tantrums the zombies have in my mind. It seems they are fine until they become agitated. That's when it seems they start to get violent and start chowing down on one another."

He paused to give me time to think over what he said. I had to concur. The occasions of violence I had witnessed had all started with annoyance, or so it seemed. I nodded my head to him in agreement.

"I think if we stay calm and steer clear, sticking together, we have a good chance of avoiding trouble." I nodded again.

"Secondly, we should head down to the grocery store and get four or five jugs of distilled water for ourselves. We will go today when we leave here, and we will keep them at my place. We can also use my place for sanctuary. It's not enough that we have water; we must eliminate the poison from the existing public water supply if we stand a chance at seeing anything normal again."

I squinted in confusion. "How do you propose we do that, Jace? I have no idea what that is going to take! Do you?"

"Well, it may be far-fetched, but if we can get into the water purification facility, we can figure out how to drain the supply. This would end the drinking of the existing tap water. Hopefully, this would give us a leg up over these freaks. If nothing else we could see what happens when they have no access to the water. I am going to grab some books about water purification. Sit here. I'll be back. If anyone starts to act flaky grab your bag and come to Stack 22."

I nodded to him that I understood and watched as he headed toward the stacks. My eyes began to immediately scan the scene before me. One of the zombies was Claire Hunt, the head librarian. Man, did she look a mess. One of her ears was obviously dangling from the weight of her earring. She lurched violently as she tried and failed to shelve books, and she was rapidly losing her patience. I was careful to not look directly at her in case she had any awareness left in her dead mind that might let her see me back. I certainly didn't want her taking a coffee break with my brains.

I continued to keep my head down, glancing up every few seconds out of the corners of my eyes. I suddenly heard a ruckus over at the stack where Claire Hunt was working. My eyes snapped over to see two male gray-faces, each tugging on Ms. Hunt's arms as though engaging in a macabre tug of war. She looked furiously angry, even in those dead, hollow eyes, and she was pulling back with all of her might. Gurgling noises and spit flew from the mouths of all three as the pulling war progressed. What had started this? Only seconds ago she was blindly shelving books. I had not witnessed her, or any one of them for that matter, doing anything that would irritate even the most impatient of souls!

Suddenly, as the battle wore on, Hunt gave a good yank to her arm in an effort to regain control. A ripping, crunching sound emitted from her body and her arm completely detached from her body. A pile of white worms, which I could only assume were maggots, fell from the socket onto the floor, squirming and writhing in the place where they landed. My stomach retched, and I let out a scream that was fit to be tied. I instantly regretted it. The three zombies' heads swung in my direction. They took notice of me, and letting go of both the remaining torso and disembodied arm, they began to make their way over to me. I froze with panic, the electric taste of bile filling my mouth. I couldn't move, though in my head I was already out the door and down the road.

Suddenly Jace was there, out of nowhere. He grabbed my arm and flung me behind his body protectively. "Grab our things and get to the closet. Run!" He shoved three large books into my arms, and, after picking up a chair, he charged at the living corpses with an almost psychotic level of violence.

I did as I was told without thinking twice. Once in the closet, I watched through the cracked door as he swung the chair erratically to and fro in an effort to hit any of them he could. When the chair connected with one of their bodies, it did little to deter them from their mission. He managed to knock each of them down once before connecting the back of the seat with Claire Hunt's face and neck. While I didn't hear a sound except for the strike, I am sure there was one. Her head flew a good ten feet, the rotting flesh she sported unable to keep it attached. It hit one of the stacks with a dull thud and fell to the floor; her body immediately did the same, lifeless and spent completely. The other two zombies looked more confused than ever and staggered back a step or two, obviously not understanding what had just taken place. It didn't take long for them to put their focus back on Jace. He was ready, and he was suddenly aware of exactly what needed to be done to win the battle.

I speculated why this zombie had maggots, and yet I didn't witness others with maggots. This stirred the question: are some rotting differently than others? Needless to say, then, it was just a matter of time until the zombies were eaten alive from the inside out; this thought alone gave me more hope.

R.W.K. Clark

CHAPTER 7

I remained in the closet, scared out of my mind. Much like watching a train wreck I could not look away from the crazy, gruesome scene before me. At first, Jace used the chair much like a lion tamer would, keeping the two stinking maniacs at bay as best he could, but he was smart; he would not allow them to back him up at all. When the opportunity presented itself, he swung hard at the zombie on his left, who I was inappropriately thinking looked a lot like Tommy Callahan from my anatomy class. The swing connected, ripping the flesh on his neck but doing little else. Jace quickly turned to Zombie number two and did the same. The left side of its skull crumbled, but the head did not give way. Something sparked my thinking: their brain was functioning, even though the rest of their body was biologically lifeless. We must detach the brain from the body! Obviously, Jace had grasped this epiphany and was running with it.

Jace aimed the chair at his second target again; the other was still in a bit of shock, I think. He was struggling to get what little wits he had about him together. When the chair hit Zombie number two in the head, it did the trick. His head tore grotesquely from his neck, ripping sickly and severing his corroded, pest-infested spine. The head hung limply down his back like a horrifying aviator's scarf, but it wasn't flying in the wind. The gray-face fell to his knees with a deafening thump! His torso fell forward, and just like that he was no more. He didn't even twitch.

Now for the last one. I found myself to be Jace's morbid little cheerleading squad from the safety of that closet, offering up mock swings and words of encouragement which he couldn't possibly hear. He took aim on the last zombie, a look of determination in his eyes like I had never seen. It took only one strike to finish the job; he had already caused enough damage to give him the advantage. The second strike not only sent the rotten head flying, but it also broke the skull completely open. It landed at the foot of the closet door, right where I stood watching. The brain had no maggots, no rot. It was pulsating with energy it should not have possessed. It was alive, yet quickly dying.

Jace let the chair fall from his hands onto the floor, where it clattered to rest. I ran sobbing from the closet into his arms. He was gasping for breath, and he looked to be in as much shock as I was.

But we had the answer; we knew how to survive as best we could.

"We have to get out of here. What set these three off?" Jace's breathing was improving, but he was covered in sweat, and his pupils were dilated like crazy.

I had no response to his question. "It was quiet. She

was busy; they were busy. It was sudden. I have no idea…"

"Let's get the bags and books, head to the store, and then make our way to my place. We can plan our next move from there." I was in agreement. I didn't want to stay in this place a moment longer. The smell which had taken over here was repulsive. Rotting flesh…

Once we had ourselves organized Jace took me by the hand and led me out the front door. The daylight was nearly blinding, causing my eyes to squint in defense. I stumbled alongside him, and once they were adjusted, I could see that the campus was literally teeming with zombies. There had to be hundreds of them! This was not the bad news, however. The bad news was the fact that every other one seemed to be fighting with, or eating, another.

My stomach continued to do its sick dance. "Act normal. Walk with your head up, Alicia. Just try to block it out; don't look." He steered me around, acting as though nothing around us was really happening. It seemed they took no notice of us, believe it or not. I just wanted to be off campus.

The scene on the city streets was no better. Everywhere they fought and feasted. Even the aisles of the grocery we entered were overwhelmed with the hungry beasts. Maggots and flesh were scattered to and fro. We managed to grab four gallons of distilled water and made our way to a checkout aisle manned by a boy of about eighteen. Half of his face was gone, and I couldn't help but think I would have called in sick to work if I were he.

He grunted a sick welcome to us and rang up the water, all the while staring right past us into nothingness. I was waiting for Jace to pay, toting my backpack on my back and a gallon of water in each hand. Jace was counting out the change that was needed, and he miscounted. The boy, whose name tag read 'Roy,' was quickly becoming irritated. I began to sweat. After what seemed like hours of nerve-racking counting and recounting, Jace threw the handful of change at the growling gray-face, grabbed the other two gallons, and we ran out the automatic doors without looking back. Ducking into an alley, we leaned against the building to catch our breath, both looking back in the direction we came from. Once we felt safe, we mutually decided to take the alleys to his place to avoid any further confrontations.

CHAPTER 8

The alley was long, stretching for blocks ahead. I was not originally from Los Angeles; while I had familiarized myself with the area pretty well, I did not know the shortcuts and alleyways at all. This was new, and I had no idea where we were going. We walked in silence for about four blocks before turning onto a regular street. It stopped in a dead end, and we went to the last house on the right. There was a wooden staircase leading up the side of it. As it turned out, this was Jace's apartment.

He let me in without saying a word. I entered and was surprised at how neat and tidy he kept his surroundings. "Do you have a housekeeper?" I was joking, but somewhere inside I knew I was serious. I had never met a male of the species who was so meticulous when it came to keeping house. There wasn't even a dirty dish in the sink!

The entry was in the kitchen. I walked about six steps and walked through a doorway which led to the living room. It was decorated in a masculine fashion: the entertainment center was created neatly out of bricks and boards; very creative and attractive! A footstool sitting before an overstuffed brown rocker was made of painted sewer pipe and lined with a faux brown fur stuffed pillow. A sofa was along the wall on the right. Wall hangings were strategically placed beneath a shelf which ran the perimeter of the room and into the next, which was a den with a computer and more seating. The shelf was lined with a beer can collection which would boggle the mind of any serious enthusiast.

"Wow, Jace. This is really nice!" I was impressed, and I wasn't about to hide it.

"Have a seat. I'm going to put the water in a safe place, unless you want a drink first, and to get cleaned up a bit, of course." He looked at me, trying to read my mind.

"That would be great." He handed a gallon to me and pointed to a door off the living room. It was a quaint little bathroom that was modestly decorated. I thanked him and entered, shutting the door behind me.

I found a washcloth and towel in the bathroom cabinet and using a bar of soap and as little of the distilled water as possible I freshened up. I found myself wishing I had brought deodorant and fresh clothes, but no sooner did the thought enter my mind than Jace knocked lightly on the door and told me there were sweats, a t-shirt, and deodorant outside the door. I thanked him and wrapped a towel around myself, so I could appropriately fetch the items. Within ten minutes I felt a thousand times better. I emerged from the bathroom, announcing, "All clear."

"I'm good for now. It's your turn," I stated as Jace

headed for the bathroom. "I figured we could research the water treatment facility and how to get the water cleaned up." The look on his face was grim, and I knew it was time to get serious.

∞

I sat down and booted up my laptop; soon he returned, and we talked all the while. There was no way to filter the tap water on such a large scale with no resources; the plan was to dump it and start from scratch, but we would need to do this with some type of filtration system for the new water. The first thing we did was research water filtration systems. If we could locate a system which could filter enough water just for the two of us to get by for a couple of days at a time, we would be set. We had to keep in mind that, while the zombies were managing to continue their day-to-day patterns like going to work, it would not be wise to make an in-store visit to get a water filter system. They had become far too violent and unpredictable to take any risk like that.

With a bit of research, we found a unit we considered ideal for our needs. The 'Indestructastill 1000' had the ability to hold twelve gallons of water while producing ten distilled gallons per day for use. It was compact and lightweight, making it the perfect option considering that we had no idea what we were facing from one day to the next. For all we knew we would have to leave L.A. at any time for our own safety. The only issue with the distillery unit was that it was sixteen hundred dollars. We were college students; need I say more?

I put my laptop on the coffee table and turned to Jace. "So, we'd better formulate a plan to get our hands on one of these babies."

Jace nodded. He was thinking hard and trying to acknowledge me at the same time. I remained still, trying to come up with my own brilliant idea. Neither of us was a shoplifter—heck, I was scared to borrow my mom's earrings without asking—plus, Jace just didn't exude a hardened criminal persona. The fact was stealing it was the only way we were going to get it, and we were both acutely aware of this fact.

"We're gonna have to steal one." He had read my mind. I nodded solemnly at him.

"That's what I figured…" My stomach felt sick.

"We can look at it a couple of different ways," he continued. "Did you ever steal candy or a toy from the store when you were a kid?"

"Me?" I felt my eyes go huge and Jace chuckled at me. "Well, you're one of the few who hasn't. There's a comparison that won't work. Okay, here is the fact: they're zombies. How aware of what we are doing are they really going to be?"

I took a breath to regain my patience. "Jace, they are aware enough to get pissed and start eating each other when they are irritated. I think that's enough for me."

He sat back on the sofa with what appeared to be exhaustion. "We have to think about this for a while."

We were silent for the next few minutes. I was supposed to be thinking about our strategy for obtaining our distillery, but the way he smelled was a major distraction. Not like cologne or deodorant, but heavenly nonetheless, like pheromones and spice. I closed my eyes and inhaled his scent more deeply. When I realized that I was subconsciously leaning toward him my eyes snapped open and I jumped up from a sitting position to my feet. How embarrassing!

"Well, we might as well get over it, because we have no choice but to steal it!" Did those words come out of my mouth? I was sure they had; they did. They were the truth, though, whether either of us liked it or not.

Jace nodded yet again. "I know." His voice was low and sober. "We need weapons. We know we have to basically knock their heads off, so as long as we have something to club them with and a lot of guts we should be fine. Listen, you are going to have to do the actual stealing; I don't want to be the only one doing the defending, but there are only two of us. I'll wield a bat; you make like a bandit."

I didn't respond because I knew this made sense, and the very thought of fighting the gray-faces alone was almost too much to handle right then. A thief I would be. I just hoped I could find it in me to be as slick and fast as I needed to be.

Now that we seemed to have a solid plan I sat back down next to him and grabbed my laptop. "What's next on the research agenda?"

Next, we researched the treatment facility and learned about the holding tanks, the layout of the facility, and how to dump the water. We printed all the information off via Bluetooth on his printer. We then investigated filtration. With a city the size of L.A., we would need extensive equipment, and it just didn't seem immediately feasible. He would continue to research a viable solution, but in the meantime, we would continue to use distilled water, walk around with baseball bats for protection (which he thankfully had), and focus on dumping the existing water supply from the city's towers so it could not be accessed. This would hopefully not only stop the spread of the bacteria, but if my theory is correct, lack of water would have the zombies dropping off like so many flies.

Super ZeroMart was a big box store that had everything money could buy, and while it did not specialize in water distillers, they had them in stock. I was really relieved that we did not have to visit a small shop; it would have been a nightmare trying to get the distillery. For one thing, it would have been kept in the back, behind the counter; this meant killing zombies right away. Second, we would have no idea how many more zombies would be in the back of a place like that. Super Zero was a gift. If you had to shoplift from zombies, you need at least thirty aisles to run around in if you want to confuse them and throw them off.

So, we bucked up and decided to head out while there was still a bit of sun in the sky. Once it was dark getting away would be easy; then we could come back, eat, rest, and eventually head for the water treatment facility with our new water distiller to execute the next step of 'Mission: Eradication.'

We made a plan to leave at three in the morning for the water treatment plant. We had a map and a strategy; I personally thought it was well planned. We would enter through an employee entrance which was kept open. We would take a specific route of corridors to the main control room, at which point we would kill any present gray-faces, barricade ourselves in, and proceed to figure out how to dump the volatile water. It was now noon, and we decided that, when we returned, we would eat and watch a movie to pass the time until we slept. Until then, we armed up with our bats, emptied our backpacks and headed out the door and to the Super ZeroMart located eight blocks from Jace's apartment.

R.W.K. Clark

CHAPTER 9

The parking lot at the Super Zero was virtually empty of cars, only one or two parked on the very outskirts of the lot being the exception. There was one zombie with scraggly red hair lurching around; it looked like he was attempting to gather shopping carts, of which there were six. He simply couldn't wrap what little there was of his brain around the task, and they remained a mess. When he tried to push one into another, he succeeded in doing nothing more than pushing the one in front ten more feet away. It was laughable, but hearing the gurgling growls which emitted from his stinking cavity of a mouth was enough to make me hold my laughter in.

We made it in, and there was only one checkout lane out of twenty open. A zombie stood at the register following a buzzing fly with its eyes, more entertained than anything. Another was trying to fold messy t-shirts in the women's clothing section. She picked up already-folded shirts one at a time, twisted them awkwardly around her hands, and put them in a pile of wadded up shirts beside her. Wow.

We made our way to hardware and plumbing

supplies and found exactly what we were looking for within minutes: the Indestructastill 1000. I might have been a woman, but I had to admit that the picture of the distillery on the box, all gleaming stainless steel, was enough to turn me on right then. I could almost smell the water!

There were absolutely no gray-faces to be seen. Jace had his bat on his shoulder, ready, but I didn't think he was even going to need it. I was scoping out our surroundings: we were in the back of the store, but I saw no emergency exits of any kind, not even the ones with alarms. I walked about ten feet away to fetch a random shopping cart from the intersection in the aisles and saw the store's third zombie, shuffling through a box of pipe fittings.

"Help?" He croaked out the question.

I shook my head, smiled politely, and answered, "No, thank you." Out of the corner of my eye, I saw Jace's head snap to attention. I took the cart and, as calmly as I could, headed back to Jace. I could feel the monster's dead eyes on me until I disappeared from sight.

Jace picked up the box and put it in the cart. We began to walk to the front of the store. "You are going to keep it in the cart. Run with the cart. It will make it so much easier for you, okay?"

I nodded at him, and right then I heard a shuffle behind us. I turned to see the zombie from the pipe aisle loping behind us, headed right in our direction. I lowered my voice, "He's on us. Let's pretend we need some other items." I no more said it than I turned down the baby section. I was surrounded by diapers and wipes. Jace wisely followed.

We kept our eyes peeled toward the aisle's end without looking directly at it, and when the gray-face appeared I grabbed a four-pack of baby bottles off the shelf, "Honey, this should be perfect for the little one while we travel. It has plastic bags which go inside, so it's sterile. Don't have to worry about washing them so much!"

"Just what we need! You have such a good eye for these things, dear." The zombie paused just long enough to observe our little exchange before shuffling off. We remained where we were until the sound of his grotesque, uneven footsteps faded into the distance, then we headed out of the side aisle, taking a sharp right and heading back to the exits at the front of the store. We picked up what other necessities we could use, slipping them into each other's backpacks. When I saw the checkout aisles come into view, my heart began to pound heavily. I could almost swear it was audible, and I looked over at Jace to see if he could hear it, but he gave no sign he could. I tried to breathe.

We made our way to the main doors, Jace holding the bat in a 'ready to strike' manner. He had his back to me, looking the store over carefully. I just got to the doors when I heard the unmistakable shriek of a gray-face, and it sounded pissed.

I took off running full-force, not even turning around to see what kind of trouble Jace had come to meet. Even though I knew no one was behind me, I could swear I felt them, that the cart zombie from the parking lot was onto me. I turned my head to glance to my rear: no one. Jace was about twenty feet behind me and gaining fast. Fifty feet or so behind him was the zombie who had followed us to the baby goods aisle; he was losing more ground than anything. I focused on getting to the alley where we had determined we would meet up if we were separated, even though he was right behind me. Might as well stick with the plan, since we had come up with no alternative.

I ran about halfway down the alley and, leaving the cart with the water distiller right in Jace's way, I ducked down behind a big red commercial dumpster. Jace snagged the cart on his way by and pushed it out of sight, behind the dumpster with me. He plopped to the ground beside me, and for the next few minutes, we focused on catching our breath and listening for zombies. Other than the sound of frighteningly light traffic and a few birds all was still. Why aren't the animals turning dead too? This thought fluttered carefreely through my head, as though it were taking a simple stroll. I felt detached from reality more than I ever had in my life.

After about ten minutes, we felt secure enough to move without confronting a gray-face. Jace stood and snatched the distillery from the cart, darted back, and sat again. "I can't believe it went so smoothly. I couldn't have hoped for better."

I don't know why, but this statement infuriated me.

Smoothly? Really? "What the heck are you talking about, Jace? My heart is still pounding. I'm scared to death! Don't you understand that he was following…" Jace's mouth suddenly covered mine with such passion and aggression that I immediately turned to butter. Wow, he tasted good. He smelled even better, and could he kiss! I was no longer in an alleyway in Los Angeles. I was floating on a chocolate raft atop marshmallows on a sea of hot cocoa. I was sliding down a rainbow made of candy. I was…

He slowly pulled away. I could tell he didn't want to, and I certainly didn't want to either. What, and face all this horrifying reality? I could honestly live without it, but I knew it was time. It took us a couple more moments to pull our eyes apart. He was smiling slightly; I was grinning like a fool. It was magnificent!

"Hi," was all he managed, and I couldn't manage a response at all. "We have a new water filter system built for two. Whew! I guess if ever there was a way to bond with someone we've found it. Not bad, Alicia."

The smile was plastered to my goofy face, and it seemed like an hour before I was able to pull myself out of my reverie, but it was mere seconds only. I shook my head back and forth to clear the cobwebs and looked down at the box on Jace's lap. "Now what?"

"Now we go back to my place, fill our bellies, and get some rest. We'll head to the water treatment plant in the morning while it's still dark, just as we planned. We can set this up in my apartment and get it running while we take care of business. There will be water ready for us sooner that way." With that, we stood up and looked up and down the length of the alley. All was clear as far as we could see. The sky was beginning to get dark; it was definitely time to go.

CHAPTER 10

Back home, or at least that was what seemed like the appropriate term for Jace's apartment, I felt so safe and secure. It was only my second visit, and I didn't want to leave again, even though circumstances dictated the opposite. I was starving and cold, even though the night was warm. It was time to grab a blanket, sit on his couch, and eat something. I felt weak and much more tired than I would have liked.

Frozen pizza was the fare for the evening, and believe it or not Jace had a bottle of merlot his sister had bought him when he moved in two years ago. He uncorked it and put on some good old-fashioned heavy metal. We ate mostly in silence, but after my second glass of wine, I began to loosen up quite a bit verbally.

"Where are you from, Jace?" I said it with a slight smile, to put him at ease.

He blushed and shook his head. "Topeka, and you?"

"Tulsa. Do you have a girlfriend waiting in Topeka?"

"No." He paused briefly. "I did, but she found she liked my best friend Matt much better."

I was at a loss for words. I changed the subject, and I was buzzed. "So, it may be the panic talking, but would you like one?"

He made eye contact with me and held it for eternity. Without saying a word he walked around the small kitchen table for two and bent down. When his lips touched mine a shock of electricity shot up and down my spine. I could not stop my arms from wrapping around his neck.

Maybe we were both frightened to death. Maybe we were a bit drunk. All I can say is that the passion with which we made love was numbing. I forgot about the zombies, the fear, and the feeling that we might not live long. I forgot about everything but Jace, his touch, and the way he made me forget. The feel of his lips and tongue on my nipples. The way his fingers played me like a violin when they were between my legs. Topeka, Kansas should be proud.

I dare say we both slept much better that night, and we didn't even need the movie to bore us into sleep. We took care of inducing good sleep all by ourselves.

∞

Even though we planned to rise at three, I found myself wide-awake at a quarter to one. Jace was already alert, sitting at the window and watching whoever was making all the racket from the street in front of his apartment building.

I crouched and walked to him, no longer wondering if I was dreaming. I peeked over the window sill. In the middle of the street were two zombies, both appeared to be men. They were violently fighting—over what we could not tell. It was an even battle, one was as strong as the other, and as the seconds ticked by I began to wonder if the screeching and tearing and punching would go on forever.

My question was soon answered. Seemingly out of the shadows gray-faces began to appear. First one came from an alley just west of the window. Soon, one emerged from a house across the way. A woman lurched in from the small park next to the house. Before long there was a dogpile of zombies ripping at each other, and within minutes limbs were flying. One torso wriggled and squirmed from just outside the group. It progressively got worse, and we watched in horror until about ten to three. Jace jerked me out of my trance with the words, "Alicia, we have to get going."

"Jace, how far are you from the city center?" It was a question I asked with purpose. If we were really close, we would never be truly safe in his apartment. The zombies would eventually find their way in, and then what? The word 'relocation' was flashing in neon in my brain.

Jace held my gaze. "About two blocks. It's not going to work, is it? Staying here, I mean. We need to set up camp in a safer place."

I nodded and looked back outside. I could see the shadowy forms of seven more zombies making their way to what was now becoming a free buffet. "We have to cut off the water supply and find a better, safer place to hole up while we wait. Staying here could very well be the death of us."

"That will be the next priority, but right now we have to gear up and make our way to the water treatment plant." Jace had gotten the still running last night; it had taken him only about a half-hour, so we could now focus on the task before us. "By the time we get back, we should have a lot more good water to use for tonight."

It didn't take either of us long to get dressed, pack our backpacks, and arm ourselves with bats. I had played softball in junior high, and I hadn't been half-bad, but times like this were enough to make you doubt your own abilities. I wondered if I could 'woman up' when it was needed.

We walked through the kitchen to the door, Jace in front of me. He didn't want me outside alone for even a second, even long enough for him to lock the place up.

"Alicia, stop." I did. He had turned to face me, and he was looking at me as if he were trying to drink me in. "I want you to know I don't just have girlfriends. I don't just have sex. I know we're under stress, but last night... I really wanted that."

The smile on my face could have easily spanned a mile.

"Me too, Jace." I looked back at him, meeting his gaze with steadfast surety. "I'm glad I'm with you. I don't know that anyone else would be a better fit... in any way."

He put his hands on my shoulders, ignoring the canvas straps which were securing my backpack so well. He leaned in, and I felt his tongue lick the length of my lips and back. I opened my mouth slightly so his tongue could explore further. At the first sign that he would, I nipped gently at it, then committed myself fully to his kiss, even using a bit of force. If this was to be the last time I tasted him, then taste him I would.

After what seemed like hours we straightened up and got our wits about ourselves. It was time to face the dead masses, the crumbling monsters which threatened our very existence from every direction.

"Are you ready, Alicia?" He looked very serious after such a great kiss.

I nodded and smiled. "I am, Jace. As ready as I'll ever be."

Jace winked at me, turned and opened the door, and there we went, into the darkness of three in the morning.

R.W.K. Clark

CHAPTER 11

The trip to the plant was uneventful, but we kept to ourselves, taking advantage of every shadow in sight. There were more gray-faces than I expected, dozens in the five miles to the plant. The time of night made it a frightening fact in and of itself. What had changed? Why were they wandering about at such a time?

The water treatment plant was a massive place. We arrived earlier than planned, and it was a good thing because we struggled to find the desired employee entrance. Once we did, things went much more smoothly than we anticipated. There were fewer zombies on the property than we thought there would be. Luckily, we encountered only one in the plant; Jace beat him down immediately. The place was a wasteland, purposefully ignored for the sake of meeting the needs of gray-faces everywhere. We were more certain than ever that we were on the right track.

We found the main control room with absolutely no problem, and within minutes of finishing our barricade, Jace located a procedural handbook. Chapter 37.N explained emergency water storage release procedures. It also let us know that the dumped water would go into the Los Angeles River. This didn't matter. The water in the river was already toxic. Until we solved the filtration problem, we would likely be robbing grocers from here to Seattle.

We set about following the steps to dump the water. It was surprisingly simple; as it began to drain from each and every tank and tower in L.A. and the surrounding area, we began to make love right there on the floor. In the heat of our passion, we almost didn't notice the barricaded door being violently struck from the other side. We almost didn't hear the screams and groans emitting from the mouths of the zombies who were on to us. But we eventually did, and we both armed up with baseball bats and bad attitudes.

"Can we speed things up?" The heat was on, and we both knew it. He had no more than opened his mouth to answer me than the door came crashing in. Chairs and the heavy desk flew as if they were made of paper. The zombies who lurched in were in bad shape. A lot of missing skin and limbs and the smell they gave off was enough to make a mortal want to commit suicide.

"No… this is the way it goes. Slow and sure." Seven zombies approached, and they looked pissed off, if indeed they had emotion. Jace ran forward full force. I was stumped as to how to proceed, but only for a moment. Aim for the head, Alicia. You are faster and smarter than they.

I charged forward as well. The first gray-face I hit found its head splattered against the wall by the door. He gave up the ghost right away. I went for the next.

He had gotten a hold of my jacket and was not letting go. Where in the heck was Jace? I spotted him for a brief moment, and he seemed to be taking monsters down right and left. I slid out of my jacket sleeves and bashed that one in like the other. Her head gave like a ripe melon. Done, and on to the next one.

After my third beast was down, I was able to come up for air. Jace had two of them on him at once, and those were just bad odds. As I made my way over to help I saw two more lurch into the control room. Gosh, give us a break!

I fought alongside Jace, beating down one who was trying to bite his arm. Fortunately he had worn leather. The horrid monsters were so putrid and rotten it took only one good strike to demolish their heads.

I moved on to the newbies that were coming through the door, and they were coming in droves. I was swinging blindly, taking them out one by one. It was easy, actually, as long as you kept your distance.

It wasn't long before the numbers really dwindled. Jace and I were able to barricade the door, reinforcing it even better than before. The water was still draining. Maybe we could win this battle after all.

We sat in two swivel chairs situated at the main control desk. Jace pulled a thermos of distilled water from his pack and offered it to me. I drank long and hard. I handed it back to him, and he proceeded to do the same.

"It looks like they don't want us to do this. We are definitely on to something," I said, with zombies screaming in pain all around us.

Jace tipped the thermos and took another swig. "I agree."

Fists began to beat on the door yet again, but this time the door will not give way so easily. Jace looked at the capacity meter. It was at a mere sixty percent. If we could keep them at bay just a little longer. I looked at the door. The barricade shook slightly, but it would not give way.

We sat in smug silence for about ten minutes watching the meter get lower and lower. The zombies had stopped pounding now. They were just screaming. Screaming in anger, screaming in pain. Screaming for the water which had spurred, and maintained, the monstrosities they had become. I had a feeling we were going to win the battle, if not the war.

∞

The smell the bodies gave off was enough to make me want to vomit. "Jace, let's move," I said, and we made our way to the other end of the control room where stood a glass wall with some sort of observation room. Perfect place to wait this ordeal out.

"So, where were we when we were so rudely interrupted?" Jace was flashing a full-fledged grin, and I found myself smiling back eagerly.

"I think we were somewhere on the floor…"

Then back to the floor we went.

Jace took full advantage of our sense of safety, vigorously caressing my body with heavy hands through my clothing. I gratefully did the same to him, fully enjoying every aspect of the way he felt, smelled, and tasted. His hands soon found their way under my shirt. I loved the way they felt on my skin, and I could swear he was leaving trails of flame wherever he touched. The zombies still screamed and snarled, but I could barely hear them. The pounding and ripping was louder, but I couldn't have cared less. If this was heaven, I was in.

I barely noticed as he slid my jeans down; I was too busy with his. Suddenly he was inside me, and I felt an overwhelming urge to laugh in a mixture of insane fear and ecstasy. I was nearly there, and as I met each and every one of his thrusts I let go. He bit down gently on my ear when he reached his peak, his entire body going stiff. A massive groan released from his lungs, and he collapsed on top of my spent body in a final expression of relinquished control.

As we lay there together listening to the monsters angrily try to conquer our barricade, Jace raised himself up onto his forearms and looked me in the eye.

"Are we good?" He was smiling. I was smiling, but I was blushing more.

I nodded. "We are absolutely great."

With that Jace gave a good, hearty laugh and separated himself from my body. I groaned in disappointment, but I knew the moment had to end. We dressed and armed ourselves before returning to the gauges. We sat in two of the chairs in the room to confer.

"So what's next, Jace?" The water supply was

draining fast now, faster than we could have anticipated. It was a relief.

"I expect that we will need to stay here until we see the clear signs of change. I mean, in their behavior. We need to see that the lack of water is having a negative effect on them, or we will be starting from square one, Alicia." I didn't answer him. There was no answer; he was right.

We sat still, doing a little bit of chatting now and then and eating beef jerky. By 8:10 a.m. the water registered as completely drained. The city's supply was depleted. By 8:45 a.m. the sound of the gray-faces began to dwindle a bit. Surely they weren't dying off already. It was my guess that they had begun to seek out alternative sources of the poison to maintain their vile conditions, and so the violent mob outside the door had thinned out. I could only hope my theory was correct.

∞

10:00 a.m. brought complete silence to the corridor outside the control center. Why didn't the designer of this building think to install a safety glass window in the door for observation? Probably because he didn't foresee a zombie apocalypse on the horizon. Regardless, we were playing it by ear, and both of us had our ears peeled.

"I'm gonna have to man up and check out the situation." Jace's voice broke through the daze I sat in.

I shook my head vigorously. "You can't just amble on out there, Jace. Just a little bit ago they filled the place up. Now you just want to walk on out there like we are the only two people left on Earth?"

"For all we know we are the only two people left on Earth. I need to investigate the situation. Or would you rather have the honors?"

I stared at him as though he had a third arm growing out of his forehead. "Of course I don't want the honors. Do what you have to do. I'm coming too… with my bat, of course."

"Of course. I wouldn't have it any other way." We both stood and crept toward the door quietly, as if we were making more noise than a bull in a china shop. Nothing could be further from the truth, but playing it safe was better than being sorry. Slowly but surely we disassembled our barricade. I was looking and listening so intently my head began to hurt, but worry was a waste of time. Nothing even attempted to get through the door. No pounding, no growling, no screaming. It was silent.

When the door was fully exposed, Jace told me to get my bat ready but stay back. I cooperated fully, and he opened the door just enough to get a good scope on the hallway outside. His head came back in, and smiling he stated, "It's all clear, Leesh." I smiled back and darted to his side. We made our way cautiously into the corridor to meet the next circumstance which would challenge us.

R.W.K. Clark

CHAPTER 12

The water treatment plant was completely empty of gray-faces, and I had a difficult time comprehending where they could have all gone all at once like that. Why would there be no stragglers? Wouldn't any of them want to stay to try to do us in? The fact was that these people were no longer people; they were dead men and women walking. Their ability to reason and plan was as dead as they were.

We got outside and took deep breaths of fresh air. No zombies to be seen.

"I think we should take Pelham Road to get back to the city center, you know, just to be safe." Jace looked serious, and his plan sounded reasonable to me. Even if the zombies couldn't use logic, seeing two people with backpacks coming into the city center from the water treatment plant couldn't be good.

The alternative route turned out to be the best idea Jace had come up with thus far. We walked Pelham Road, and when we got about five miles from the actual outskirts of the city. Jace took notice of a small house behind a row of trees.

"Let's go knock on the door. Why would zombies

need lights? Maybe we will find someone who's normal. They may need us." Jace took my hand and tugged me in the direction of the small country home.

We got close enough for me to get a sinking feeling in the pit of my stomach; there in the driveway, next to a sedan with the driver door wide open, was a person lying on the ground. As we got closer, it became obvious the person was dead. It was a woman, chubby, but small in stature. Her neck was ripped open, and her skull had been caved in. Her brain hung out the gaping hole; a large bite had been taken from it.

I was in shock. This was a first. Since when had the gray-faces gone to such an extreme? "Did the zombies do this?"

Jace appeared to be as surprised as I felt. "I don't know, Alicia, but I think it's safe to say that a coyote or wolf had no part. They wouldn't bother to crack open the shell to get the nut out."

We stared a few moments longer. Jace climbed into the sedan and tried the engine. "Out of gas. The body is fresh. The car ran itself dry. Let's check out the house."

Hand-in-hand we made our way up the walk that ran from the front door to the driveway. The door was locked, forcing Jace to jog back to the car and fetch the ring of keys from the ignition. There was only one key that resembled a residential door key, and it worked like a charm. Jace opened the door, and we stepped into the air-conditioned interior of the home.

It was small but nicely furnished and clean. The living room was the first room we encountered. Off to the right was the master bedroom and straight ahead was a doorway which led to the kitchen/dining room. To the left was a hallway with four doors running along either side; bedrooms, of course. As it turned out, there were two small fully-furnished bedrooms, one of which was being used as an office, a bathroom with light pink accents, and a linen closet. Everything was working.

I wandered into the kitchen and looked more closely around. The kitchen was spotlessly clean, the dish strainer sporting only a saucer, glass, and fork. Everything was wiped to shining. In a small alcove-type area was a compact washer/dryer all-in-one unit. An empty clothes basket sat on top of it, bottom-side up.

To the right of those appliances featured a small corkboard which was fashioned to look like a washboard. Five small pieces of paper were push-pinned to the board. "Anna sees Dr. Hilliard on August 8, 2015, at 10:00 a.m." was printed on a business card. "Call Judy 8 p.m. Thurs." was scrawled on the torn corner of a piece of wide-ruled notebook paper. The others sported similar notes.

The dining table was oak, round in design, with matching high-backed chairs. An ecru doily embellished the table; an ivory-colored ceramic dish sat in the middle of the doily.

The refrigerator was completely full. Everything from cold cuts to cheeses and milk was inside. The freezer had chicken, chops, and one package of steaks. My stomach grumbled loudly and painfully. I didn't have time to worry about food right now.

Jace came around the corner. "Alicia, have you seen any sign of two people or more living here? I have only found clothes for a woman, no one else."

"I haven't seen anything out here that would answer that question, except maybe the fact that the house is immaculately clean." I cast my eyes over it once again. "Looks like a woman's house to me."

Jace walked over to a window at the rear of the kitchen, looking intently outside. I sidled up beside him. The backyard was fenced in, grassy, and it was obviously just forest beyond it. The nearest house in sight was so far up the road that you could see only the blue-gray roof hovering over the tall grass-line.

As if by ESP we both turned and walked out the front door. He went one way and I the other. We circled the house, taking in full view of our surroundings.

There was nothing for miles. It looked like we had found our base of operations. If nothing else, we found our new home.

CHAPTER 13

We figured the woman, whose name we discovered from postal items to be Belinda Smythe, had been caught unawares by a zombie who evacuated the water treatment plant. Once we had determined with a bit of surety that we were safe, we retreated back into the small house, where Jace and I fortified the points of entry with strategically rearranged furnishings. A small back door to the rear of the kitchen was the door of choice for us when it came to any future coming and going. We barricaded it as minimally as possible without compromising safety.

Next, we went to the kitchen. I let Jace boot my laptop; if Miss Smythe didn't have Internet access, we could use the hotspot on my cellular phone. It turned out she had no web access, so he proceeded to get things up and running according to Plan B. thankfully. I scavenged through the fridge and cupboards until I had gathered the makings of a good meal, and I went about preparing it while Jace went about surfing the web for any available recent news regarding the gray-faces or the possibility that anything was being done about it. It did no good; everything online was at a virtual standstill. So far, aside from Miss Smythe in the driveway, we seemed to be the only normal people around for miles.

I made a simple supper of hamburgers and potato chips with canned baked beans. It tasted simply gourmet, and by the way, Jace moaned with every bite he thought so too. We talked little as we ate, but afterward, he picked up the conversation right away.

"I am going to go outside in a bit and move Miss Smythe's body and give her a proper burial. It's too strange that they resorted to violence on a living human being. She was so far out here in the sticks, I can't imagine that little woman doing much of anything to instigate an annoyance in one of those animals. I just don't want any of them coming around just because there is a corpse lying out in the open." He had a very grim look on his face, and I had to agree, even though I had no idea why. I just didn't want them thinking this was the local café if they were eating live people now.

"What do you think spurred this on, Jace?" My voice was shaky, giving away the intense fear that was building up in my heart.

"I don't know, but here's my idea. At my place, I have a microscope kit my dad got me for high school graduation. It's a high-quality setup, with all the accessories. I'm going to grab that, the new distillery machine, some clothes, and some other useful items. I have a great big duffel bag that should be able to get the stuff here safely; I'll look in the garage to see if there is any gas in a can, you know, for a mower. If I can get Miss Smythe's car running, I will feel better. Either way,

I will leave when it's good and dark to be a bit safer."
This concerned me, Jace venturing to his apartment
alone, but the truth was we would need as many
resources as possible, and that included the water filter
system we had gone to so much trouble to steal. I could
use a good scrubbing, that much I knew, and I was
dying for a drink of good, cold water.

We hung out and talked about some of the
possibilities which could have incited a zombie to eat a
living human. We were both stumped when it came to
the science and the details, but we both agreed it must
have had something to do with the water supply being
drained. It was too much of a coincidence that we
drained the water and then subsequently discovered a
fresh human corpse so close to the water treatment
facility. We might have been wrong, but that was all we
could come up with for the time being.

∞

Around 8:15 p.m. Jace went out with a flashlight and
dug through the garage. He located about two and a half
gallons of gas in a small five-gallon can next to a push
mower, which he put into the car right away. It turned
over immediately, its sewing-machine engine sounding
top-notch. As he fastened his seat belt, I leaned in the
driver's side window.

"Jace, please…" My voice drifted off. I didn't even
want to say it out loud; I didn't want to speak the worst
into existence.

He nodded and looked me right in the eye. "I'll be

careful, Alicia. I'll be extra careful. This car is going to make things so much easier. I'll run right into anyone who is coming at me."

I smiled grimly to show him I trusted him. He continued, "Now when you go back in the house close all the vertical blinds; make sure they are turned upward so lights can't be seen from the street. Close the drapes. Make sure all the doors are locked and blocked, just like we did it earlier, okay?" I didn't answer. I was turning everything he said over in my mind. "Okay, Alicia?" He snapped me out of it with his tone.

"Okay, Jace. I'm on it." He smiled and sighed with relief. "Now, I'll be back before you know it, Cutie." I couldn't help but smile back. "Go on in. I'm not leaving until I know you are safe inside."

I knew he had limited gas until he got to a station, so I turned and bolted nervously into the house. I locked the back door behind me and slid the heavy oak china hutch we were using for a barricade back into place. I then turned the vertical blinds upward and closed the curtains, just like Jace told me to. I then went to the living room, where I waved out the window at him. He slowly started to back out, and I fixed the blinds and curtains on that window as well.

As I went from room to room repeating the tasks I couldn't help but think. What if Jace didn't come back? The thought sent a chill of terror through my body. I was hardly equipped to be alone in such a situation. While I was certainly smart enough, I just was not the quick thinker in emergency situations that Jace was.

What would I do? Where would I go? The thoughts prompted me to finish fixing the windows that much faster. I grabbed my cell and sat down in a stuffed rocker in the living room and attempted to dial my parents. They had been on vacation overseas and were due back three hours ago. Maybe they would be okay.

The phone rang and rang, but I got no response. That was the house phone, however, so I still had hope. Next, I called my dad's cell; it went right to voicemail. My moms did the same. My stomach sank; this was not a good sign. They never let their phones go dead or shut them off. They were too worried they would miss a call from me.

I leaned my head against the back of the rocker and forced myself to breathe. I began to reason with myself: I had no idea what was going on. For all I knew my parents had holed themselves up for safety, and they were fine. I made a solid decision to not worry; it would get me nowhere, only make things worse.

I stood and turned on the television set: nothing. I began to flip through the channels and finally came to CNN; miraculously it was on the air. I turned up the volume just in time to hear this:

"...though we are locked up here in the studio. The CDC announced fourteen hours ago that the situation was, and is, rapidly deteriorating. Stay indoors; we have had no further word from them since, and until we receive such we will continue to recommend that no one, I repeat, no one, leave the safety of their homes or other accommodations. This is Richard Stanley with

CNN. Stay tuned in for updates on the situation as we receive them."

The remote control fell from my hand, and I began to cry.

CHAPTER 14

I must've cried myself to sleep. I dreamed I was with Jace by the city center. We were leaving his apartment, and as we made our way to Miss Smythe's sedan, we discovered it was gone.

"That's right." Jace turned to me and spoke in the darkness. "We rode our bikes, remember?"

Bikes? Even in the dream that sounded ridiculous. I didn't own a bike. Did Jace? We began to look for our bikes when out of the darkness emerged a massive gray-face, a man of about six-foot-eight, and he looked just as wide to me. His face and shirt were covered with blood and gore, and he was smiling with glee. Why was it so dark? Where were the street lights?

Before I could even open my mouth to scream, he had a hold of Jace. Within a split second, he was biting into his cheek. Jace screamed loudly, fighting and struggling, but he was no match for the soulless monster. The zombie took Jace's head in both hands and squeezed. His skull gave way with a grotesque pop! The monster got comfortable on the tarmac and began feasting on his fresh, warm brains.

I jerked awake violently, and after running to the

bathroom I threw up everything in my stomach, even dry-heaving for what seemed like an hour after the remainder of my dinner was no more.

What was that noise? I heard something bang toward the back of the house. My stomach lurched again, but this time in sheer terror. I was holding my breath, afraid that whatever was trying to get in would hear it and become even more determined to gain entry. Had I forgotten to close one of the blinds? I exhaled slowly and began to crawl out of the bathroom on all fours, gaining only an inch at a time in my fright.

"Bang!" There it was again. I strained to hear something, anything, that would clarify who was outside. "Alicia, it's Jace! Hurry up and let me in!"

I jumped up quickly and ran to the kitchen where I proceeded to push the china hutch out of the way. I peeked through the blinds to see Jace looking anxiously about in the darkness, his arms were laden with two large canvas bags and the box containing the distillery. I undid the chain, flipped the deadbolt, and turned the knob lock. As I opened the door, Jace fell into the house. He was sweating profusely, and his eyes were wide with fear.

"Hurry, let's get this place locked back up!" He dropped his bags, put the box on the kitchen table, and within seconds we had the barricade back in place. Jace plopped into a chair around the table, spent and trying to catch his breath.

"Jace, you scared the living daylights out of me! Are you okay? What happened? Did everything go smoothly?" He seemed to nod and shake his head at the same time. I sat across from him and tried to contain my anxiety until he was in the proper condition to communicate.

After about five full minutes he looked up at me. "Things have changed more than we thought, Alicia."

I said nothing; I just waited for him to elaborate, keeping my eyes on him the entire time. He had a look on his face that told me he was replaying whatever events had taken place during his absence, trying to make as much sense of it as he possibly could.

"They are dying." He finally began to speak, and he made sure I was paying attention by maintaining eye contact.

What he said didn't click with me right away. "Who is dying?" I was confused. Weren't they already dead? Did he find others like us, others who had not been drinking the water?

He appeared to be getting a bit frustrated. "The zombies, Alicia. The zombies are dying!"

I stared at him. "How do you know? How can you be sure?"

"Well, as I was driving into town they were just everywhere; in the middle of the streets, along the sidewalks, everywhere! I noticed this one walking ahead of the car, directly in front of me, so I slowed down. You know, I didn't want to get his attention at all. I was about twenty feet behind him when he suddenly just... fell down! He didn't trip, didn't stumble, he just... fell!" He paused long enough to take a breath before continuing. "I had to stop the car. I didn't want to run him over, I mean there were so many of them I would've been dinner if I had, and Alicia, there were a few bodies, real bodies, lying around, too."

"Jace! So what about the zombie that fell?" I was getting frustrated; he was all over the place, and I was having a hard time keeping up with him.

He shook his head as if he could not believe the pictures floating around inside of it. "Well, the zombies that were walking just kept going. He didn't matter. I waited for him to move. I thought it was a setup or something like they're smart enough to set me up." He shook his head again. "After like ten minutes I went up to the body and, well, he was dead, Alicia. I kicked at him, and he just seemed to fall apart. So I got back in the car and kept going. Within the next mile, I watched five more of them do the exact same thing."

"It's the water, Jace." That was all I could say. I knew it as sure as I knew my own name.

He nodded. "Yes, but I'm pretty sure the lack of water is why they are eating any living person they can find. I don't know how that would fix things for them, but I can think of no other reason. It was like they were on a mission and nothing could deter them."

"What happened, Jace? Why do you think this? You know something you are not telling me." He continued to look in my eyes, as though he weighed out the odds on whether I would come unglued if he shared the next bit of information with me.

"When I got to the Lucky Star Mart on Melrose I

decided to gas up because there were so few of the gray-faces around there. I pulled the car up to the pump and started to put gas in. I don't think I got five gallons into that car and they started to come at me. It was nothing like it has been. It was like they… smelled me, Alicia, and they were licking their lips; they were hungry."

I didn't know what to say; my blood had gone cold, and my entire body felt frozen. They had made game of the living. We took the water, and now they wanted our blood.

At least, that was how it looked. "What are we going to do, Jace?" I tried to keep the panic out of my voice. He was just as scared as I, and we needed to think and reason properly.

He was silent for longer than I would've liked, but I knew he needed to think. Finally he said, "I am going to set up the microscope and other lab stuff I brought from my place. I'm going to turn the office back bedroom into our lab for the time being. I took some of the flesh from the dead zombie. It's in a baggy in my duffel. I'm also going to take another water sample from here if anything is in the tank. Miss Smythe's body should also be helpful; I collected a sample of her tissue before I buried her. We are going to test everything we can get our hands on. There has to be something that can give us some kind of specific idea why the zombies have changed their behavior."

"But right now I am going to get the still up and running again. I need to clean up, I'm thirsty, and I'm sure you are too. The water inside was done, so we can transfer that to some clean containers. Try to see what you can find around here. The sooner we get more water filtered, the better."

Thankful to have something to think about other than our current situation I jumped up from my chair and began to go through the cupboards. Over the refrigerator were two smaller cupboards which held large old-fashioned glass milk bottles, the kind with plastic rings around the neck for carrying. There were seven of them in all.

"Look, Jace. Will these do?" He gave me a broad smile.

"Perfect. Bring them into the back room. I have the still set up back there already." I took them down from the shelves one by one and carried them to the back bedroom. Jace filled each one, seven gallons in all. There were still three gallons remaining in the tank of the still, so I went back out and fished around the kitchen. I found a five-gallon ice cream container. Man, she must have loved her ice cream, I thought. It held the rest of the water fine. We covered the mouths of the milk bottles with aluminum foil to keep the water as clean as possible. We were able to fit two of the gallon bottles into the refrigerator but no more, so we lined the rest of the containers up neatly on the kitchen counter.

"Take one of those into the bathroom and get cleaned up if you like," Jace told me. "I'm going to use this juice pitcher to fill the still back up. It's only a half-gallon so it will take a few trips. You may as well take advantage of the time. I'll go after you."

I had never been more grateful, and thanking him, I grabbed one of the bottles and made my way to the hall closet, where I grabbed a washcloth and towel from the shelves. "I'll be out soon," I told him.

"Take your time, Alicia. Don't rush. I'm not going to." He smiled again and carried his second pitcher of water to the back bedroom.

I washed my hair, using very little soap so rinsing would not be an issue. I then cleaned my body thoroughly by wetting the cloth and soaping it up with a bottle of body wash Miss Smythe had owned. It was cucumber-scented. I felt sad using it and thinking about this dead woman who enjoyed the scent of cucumbers, just like I did.

When I was finished, I emerged from the bathroom with a towel around me. The thought of putting the same filthy clothes back on was repugnant. "Did you bring anything to wear that might fit me? A t-shirt maybe?" Jace was sitting in the rocker I had fallen asleep in, and he jumped up immediately.

"Absolutely, yep. I have a t-shirt and sweats. You will have to go without underwear, that is unless you want to wear a pair of my jockeys."

I burst out laughing. It felt so good to really laugh. "I think I'll pass, but thanks anyway." He made his way to the master bedroom, and when he came out, he had the clean clothes. As he handed them to me, his fingers brushed against mine, giving me goosebumps. I blushed, and he smiled. As I held the clothing to my chest his face got serious, and he came nearer to me.

Before I knew it his soft lips were on mine, his tongue licking, seeking out mine. I gave it to him; the kiss lasted forever, and it eliminated the fear and stress we had been burdened with for hours.

"I'm going to wash up," Jace whispered. I saw that he was blushing too, and as he made his way to the bathroom, he walked backward, keeping his eyes on me and the smile on his face.

"Watch the end table, Jace!" He moved in the nick of time, avoiding a good bruise by only seconds.

"Don't go anywhere, Alicia." He winked at me. "I'll be back soon."

CHAPTER 15

Regardless of our circumstances that night with Jace in that little country house was easily the best night of my life. While he got cleaned up, I heated up a can of beef stew, which we ate in silence with mp3 music playing softly from Jace's little unit. We stared at each other with visual caresses; words were not needed.

Afterward, we went into the living room and sat on the sofa at the far end. I took an afghan, which hung over the back of the couch, and covered up a bit with it, snuggling against Jace as a hint that I needed some human contact. He wrapped his left arm around me and kissed my forehead. I closed my eyes and reveled in the pleasure his lips gave. He began to gently kiss my entire face with sweet, light kisses which felt like feathers brushing against my skin. A soft moan escaped my lips, and I melted into his arms.

He began to caress me gently with his hands, stroking my arms and neck, finally making his way to my breasts. My nipples were already rock-hard with anticipation. I felt him smile when his fingers touched them. I opened my eyes and looked at him. He looked back at me and slowly removed my t-shirt, maintaining our look the entire time.

"I love you, Alicia. I would die for you." He kissed me full on the mouth, and there was no hesitation when my mouth opened to receive it. After a moment he began to kiss my neck, my chest, my breasts. My entire body was on fire, my hips arching involuntarily, looking for something that wasn't yet there. As if on cue his hand found its way between my legs. He gently stroked me through the sweatpants.

"Oh, Jace, I love you too." I realized my hips were moving with a bit of frenzy, and I reached down to give the string on the sweatpants a tug. They needed to come off.

Jace beat me to it, and in seconds we were both enjoying each other's nakedness with bare-faced ecstasy. I felt him thrust gently, and he was inside of me. I groaned with pleasure. Surely I should feel guilty for enjoying my life when the world was falling apart around me, but I felt no such emotion. I didn't want this to ever end.

We moved together in perfect rhythm until the warmth of my climax encompassed me. I heard him catch his breath, his body going tense. We came together, holding hands and breathing hard. I fell asleep almost immediately, with Jace still inside of me, his warm, damp skin touching mine.

∞

I woke with a start; Jace was gone. "Jace? Jace!" I jumped up, wrapping the afghan around my naked body. "Where are you?"

Jace appeared in the hallway, smiling. "Sorry, Alicia. I couldn't sleep; so much to do, so much on my mind. You were sleeping like a baby. I didn't have the heart to wake you." I fell to the couch and tears of relief seeped from under my eyelids.

"Don't do that again, Jace. I can't lose you…" My voice was a bit wracked, my tears obvious in it.

"Oh, honey, I'm sorry!" He quickly came to my side and sat down next to me, wrapping his arms around me in a secure embrace. "I would never leave without waking you and telling you what I was doing. I'm not going to leave you to deal with these things alone. I love you, Alicia." It took a bit for me to gather myself. Once I felt emotionally stable, I told him I was going to get dressed.

"I've been in the back room… er, the lab." He grinned. "I was taking advantage of the time to look over those samples I took while I was gone, as well as the water from here and… Miss Smythe."

I grimaced. "Have you found anything new?"

"I'm not sure 'new' is the word, but different definitely fits." He was still smiling as he spoke, which eased my stress quite a bit. "Go ahead and get dressed. Meet you back there."

He left the room, and I put my sweats and t-shirt back on. I stopped in the bathroom and ran a comb, which I found next to the washbasin, through my hair. When I felt a bit more satisfied with my appearance, I went to the back room to find out what Jace had discovered.

When I entered the bedroom, I noticed that Jace had clearly set up a pretty functional workspace. He removed all the knickknacks and freed the shelves now lined with tubes, beakers, and equipment... wow, Jace had brought all this from his apartment? He had a small desk lamp illuminating a card table which held his microscope, slides, and other equipment he felt we might need. He had pushed a small nightstand over to a position on his right, and on it, he had several notebooks, as well as a couple of heavy volumes I could not make out the titles to. He had our laptop set up on the desk with notebooks and plenty of pencils and a stack of more heavy volumes.

"I'm definitely going to need you," he said with smiling enthusiasm. "I'm able to identify and recognize a chemical reaction, but as to its potential effect on living tissue, well, I'm at a loss."

"What do you have?"

The look on his face told me he was not sure where to begin. "For starters, I tested the tissue from the zombie I saw die. I was unable to identify any bacteria of any kind; it's almost like the flesh is... sterile."

"Sterile?" I turned this over in my mind. The only way I could see this being true is by comparing their dead flesh to ash, or possibly dust, but I was leaning toward ash. "What about Miss Smythe's tissue? Did you find anything there?"

He nodded vigorously. "I did. There are low levels of the bacteria in her tissue. This tells me that when we turned the water off the gray-faces began to seek out living organisms which could provide them with the maintenance fix they so needed."

I was apt to agree with him. No other explanation made any sense. Could they smell it in their victims? Had Miss Smythe ingested enough of the bad water for it to build up before she could take no more of it, driving her to stop drinking it? Had we? I thought back to when I began to notice the putridity of the water. How much had I actually drunk before resigning myself to the fact that, for me, the water was undrinkable? I couldn't recall. At the time I didn't think it mattered.

Jace continued. "So I have an idea that may help us clear things up a bit. It's dangerous, and you're probably not going to like it, but I'm pretty sure it's going to be the only way to gain the clarity we are looking for."

I was afraid to ask. I took a deep breath, but I was already sure I knew what Jace was going to say. "Go ahead."

"I need tissue from a mobile, 'living' zombie. We need to find out if they have active bacteria in or on them, and if so, what the levels are. It would be ideal to have two or three varying samples for the sake of comparison." I was staring hard at him, trying to deduce whether or not this gorgeous man before me had completely lost his mind.

"Jace, how do you propose we are going to get these samples? Pick them up on sale at the Super ZeroMart?" I could taste the panic rising up in my throat. Was he serious?

He got up and walked over to me, where he knelt before the wooden chair I was seated in. He put his hands on my knees and looked me in the eye. "Alicia, we have to. If we can determine with certainty that the bacteria is the problem, we can look for a way not only to eradicate it, but we may be able to develop some sort of a vaccine that can help those who are not too far gone yet. I mean, when you look at the big picture it's sort of our responsibility, don't you think?"

I stood. His hands fell limply from my lap as it disappeared. I stared into space turning over everything he had said to me in my brain. "So do you have any bright ideas as to how we are going to get these coveted samples?" He was right; it was our responsibility. What he said was true. I saw no other way.

"Well, I plan to drive around until I am able to get one of the gray-faces alone. If I can bash it in the head just enough to knock it over, that would be perfect. Then I could get a 'living' sample. As living as it could be, anyway." He was smiling with absolutely no humor.

I shook my head. "You are not going to attempt this venture alone, Jace. This is most definitely a two-man job. I will have to help, and there are no two ways about it. That way if you have one down and he tries to attack while you gather the sample I can take him out completely." I got quiet with thought. "Wait a minute. The zombie who you took the sample from, who died. He had been going without water for the last day and a half. If we bash the heads of the living ones in and harvest samples immediately we should be safe to get quality tissue samples. Maybe we can even get lucky enough to get one who has just fed on a human."

"We can take a cooler with ice to keep the samples fresh. Miss Smythe has a small beer cooler in the garage. We will need to make some clean ice; we don't want to use anything that has been contaminated in any way." He was nodding, more to himself than to me.

"We can get started when evening falls. I will have a look at the things you already have and see if I can pick up anything you may have missed. I need to get started. We can rest throughout the daylight hours." I walked over to the chair at the card table and had a seat. "Okay, Jace. Tell me what is what, and show me your notes. Catch me up to where you are."

He pulled the wooden chair over beside me and started explaining his research from the beginning. It was good, but biologically speaking he had missed some tricks. I guess it was more than mere coincidence that two zombie survivors were chemistry and biology majors. I was beginning to believe in destiny more and more, and it filled me with courage and a sense of purpose.

It was time for me to step into my destiny.

R.W.K. Clark

CHAPTER 16

The next night we followed through with our plan to gather tissue samples from actual active gray-faces. We left our new homestead at 8:30 p.m. on the nose, and we drove around the outskirts of L.A., working our way inward and looking for any lone zombies we could find. Someone was smiling on us, because we ended up with a sample from seven different zombies. Not only did we get to bash their brains in, but we also got two samples from each one: skin and tissue, for a total of fourteen. We packed each properly, using household items from Miss Smythe's, and we put them on ice in a little cooler to keep until we got back to the house.

Our testing validated our suspicions: the bacteria levels in each zombie varied. The ones who had managed to find, and eat, living people had much higher levels than those who we found wandering or who had not found prey in recent hours. We both agreed that the bacteria was indeed the culprit. Dumping the water supply had been a smart move. Dead zombies littered the city like so much waste. Most of those remaining were covered in either bloodstains or fresh blood from eating recently. There were also more remains of living humans than we would have liked to see. They all must have panicked and gone into hiding. That would explain why neither of us saw or came into any kind of contact with any of them.

∞

The next six weeks were spent mostly within the confines of the house, reading research books we had taken from the public library and conducting a variety of experiments as we tried to find both a cure for those who were still walking around as well as develop a chemical to battle the existing bacteria. The rivers and lakes were highly polluted with the nasty little monsters, as we had quickly learned during our research. We deduced that developing the right chemical mixture, which would have to be non-toxic to humans and wildlife and then putting it into the water in L.A., would help us to get a leg up and begin to set things right again.

There was a problem with a vaccine, we soon discovered. Those who were already gray-faces had decayed on such a rapid basis that ridding them of the bacteria would just kill them off. Their organs were no longer able to sustain life. The only hope for rebuilding this society would be to find those who had not turned, had not been eaten, and whose bodies had enough of the bacteria that it needed to be eradicated. Thus far neither Jace nor I had come across anyone, and the bodies of the living were becoming harder and harder to find. We kept our focus on the chemical warfare that we believed would help us to set things right. We would pay more attention to the vaccine if, and when, the need arose.

Both Jace and I had gone to exhaustive efforts to locate any of our family members who might have still been living, all to no avail. Cell phones went right to voice mail. House phones delivered nothing but rapid busy signals. We tried a new member daily, only to become more and more discouraged with each failed attempt. We took turns crying, venting, and otherwise being held by the other until the tears would disappear, only to repeat the process again in a day or two. It was beginning to look like the only hope for the world, and for its renewing, would be us, and so with all of that in mind, we continued our research.

∞

During our seventh week of study, on a Wednesday, I was reading up on various antibiotics and how they attack different bacterial life forms. I was in the living room, and Jace was experimenting with chemicals and infected water in our makeshift little lab. Suddenly he burst into the room.

"Alicia, I think I'm really onto something here!" My heart began to beat so hard and fast I thought it would burst through my chest. We had been working nearly non-stop for so long, and lately, I felt drained and tired. Jace had told me I looked pale, and I had even been struggling to hold down food. Finding the right mix would mean getting outside and getting some real sun, which is what I figured was my entire problem.

I quickly sat up on the couch where I had been reading. "What did you find, Jace?" My voice was filled with hope.

"I combined our chemical J675 with seven parts erythromycin. At first, it didn't look like the two could sustain compatibility, but after ten minutes the erythromycin levels had not only doubled, but the molecules seemed to… grow muscles!" I must have looked at him as though he were mad, because that was exactly what I was thinking. "Never mind that. I put the combination into a water sample, dropped it on a slide, and took a look. The water sample was loaded with bacteria, and nasty ones at that. Alicia, within thirty seconds every last trace of bacteria was wiped out completely!"

I just stared at him, trying to see if all of our studies had driven him off the deep end. "I need to see the slide, Jace."

He led me excitedly to the back room where I sat at the card table and waited as he repositioned the slide. I took a hard look. The water was cleaner than any I had ever seen before. I could not even identify any medicinal molecular structures within the sample!

"Jace, I need to see this for myself. Can you set up another raw sample?"

He nodded eagerly. "I was hoping you'd ask." He got out another set of slides and put a contaminated water sample on it. Sliding it under the viewer, he stated, "Take a look."

It had to be the most disgusting sample ever. Even the earlier samples were not this bad. Things had gotten progressively worse. I hoped he was right!

"Now, give me just a second," said Jace. He removed the slide and exposed the sample. He took a dropper of light bluish liquid from a beaker on his home Bunsen burner and introduced not quite a drop onto the slide. Putting it back together he placed the sample under the viewer. "Quick, look again!" His eyes were on fire.

I bent over and looked. The new molecules were simply feasting on the bacteria; they were literally disappearing, leaving nothing behind but clear, clean molecules of water. I inhaled sharply.

"Jace, I think you're onto something, babe!" I looked again. The sample was completely clear of bacteria, and it had taken place in under two minutes.

Jace nodded vigorously. "Now all we need to do is make sure the effect is lasting. Let's get a bite to eat and come back in a while." He left things at room temperature to simulate nature as best as possible; we didn't want to deviate.

∞

While I wasn't hungry, I prepared two bologna and cheese sandwiches and gave Jace a bowl of cottage cheese with his. My appetite just wasn't what it used to be. Was I turning?

"I'm almost too excited to eat, but I know I need my strength." The look on his face changed to one of concern when he looked over at me. I had begun to pick my sandwich apart, but I had yet to take a bite. "Alicia, you have to eat."

"I'm just not very hungry, ever…," I said, my voice trailing off. "I'm worried, Jace. Do you think I'm turning?"

"No! There is no way. You haven't drunk bad water. You haven't been attacked. There is no way. We have been here for more than a month and a half. Think about what you're saying in comparison to what science says."

He was right. Whatever was wrong with me, it had nothing to do with my becoming a gray-face. A cold, maybe? The flu?

Suddenly Jace brought up a valid point. "You know, we stay here in the house, and all we do is research bacteria and screw. When was your last period, Alicia? I'm asking because you haven't had one since we've been here, as far as I'm aware."

It was like he hit me in the chest. Did I really miss something as vital as the fact that I hadn't had a period in nearly eight weeks? How could I overlook such a thing? I knew that anxiety could distract, but this was ridiculous.

"Since before the zombies, Jace…"

He smiled. His thoughts were almost audible. I was pale, had no energy, and my appetite was almost non-existent. All we did was have sex and conduct research. Yes, I was pregnant. Suddenly there was absolutely no doubt in my mind as to why I had felt so… off.

"Jace, we cannot bring a child into this!" A stricken look came over his face, a look akin to panic.

"Whatever you are thinking, you will put out of your mind immediately. For all we know we are all that is left to get things started again. There is no better time to kick things off than the present, wouldn't you say?" The joy had left his eyes. He had become enraged at the thought of terminating a pregnancy for any reason, even one like the state of the world. "I'll get you a pregnancy test from the city tonight. I'll also grab some iron pills and vitamin supplements… and more dehydrated milk. Might as well get ready to be a mom. I have a feeling it's a done deal." He stood and left the room without finishing his food.

I looked down at my own plate, guilt washing over me. Had I really just toyed with the thought of killing my own baby? He was right. This child was a new beginning, if indeed I was pregnant. I knew it was true deep inside, and I was ashamed at the level of selfishness I had just displayed. I stood and dumped my sandwich into the garbage. I needed to go find out if Jace and I were on the right track.

Especially now.

R.W.K. Clark

CHAPTER 17

I walked into the back room to find Jace kicking back in the chair at the card table, a self-satisfied look glued to his face. "It maintained, Alicia. It maintained."

I smiled broadly. It looked like we had come up with the beginning of a solution. Now to determine, and take, the next step that would bring our world back around.

"Do you have any theories as to what should be next?" I was very eager to hear what had been rattling around in Jace's mind in the last few minutes.

He continued to smile. "Yep. Sure do." He got up and went out of the room. I sat in the wood chair and waited for his return. Soon, he was back with a water bottle which contained contaminated water. It was one of many we had taken from the river so we could conduct our research conveniently. He sat at the desk and took one last look at the slide in the microscope. He smiled again, satisfied, before cleaning the slide with disinfectant. Next, he took a clean dropper and drew a bit of the contaminated water from the bottle. He prepared it on a slide and took a look. It must have been bad, because he cringed visibly.

"Take a look," he said as he rose from his chair to make room for me.

I positioned myself before the microscope and, taking a deep breath, looked at the sample. While the water looked fine to the naked eye, the microscope told another story: it was as rancid as it smelled.

"Bad," was the only word I could manage to say. Just looking at it made me want to vomit in response to my retching belly.

He nodded. "So, now that we have verified that the entire contents of this bottle, which is sixteen fluid ounces, is terribly contaminated, I will introduce the antibiotic chemical mix. I will start with one drop."

Once he had administered the drop, we let it sit for a moment, not saying a word to each other. Jace set a kitchen timer we had found in the other room for two minutes. His foot tapped anxiously while we waited for what seemed like an eternity.

Finally, the buzzer went off. We both jumped even though we expected it. Jace stopped the noise and grabbed a clean dropper from a box that held around a dozen of them. He drew some of the water and placed a drop on a clean slide he had ready and waiting. Next, he placed it under the microscope and took a look. I was holding my breath as I stared at him, waiting to see the look on his face.

He turned to me slowly. "Alicia, it shows a dramatic difference…"

I jumped up and took a look for myself. The sample was half as nasty as the first.

"Let's give it two more minutes and see what happens," I suggested. He nodded in agreement and set the timer.

This time we were ready when the timer buzzed, both of us pacing in circles in the small room. "You do the honors," Jace said to me, smiling.

I leaned over and took a look. It appeared to be worse.

"The bacteria are reproducing, Jace. Let's start from scratch and introduce two drops of water. Trial and error, right?" He took a look for himself, nodded, and began to clean droppers and slides with disinfectant.

Two drops did significantly more damage to the bacteria in a new bottle of contaminated water, but we ended up scrapping that one as well. The third sixteen-ounce bottle got four drops, just to be safe. After the two-minute timer went off, we both took a good gander.

The water was spotlessly clean!

"Woo-hoo!" Jace yelled. He jumped around, and I couldn't help but join him. We danced, we cried, we held hands, and we held each other. It looked like there was a light at the end of the tunnel.

Jace stopped and held me at arm's length. "Okay, Leesh, this is the plan. Tonight I go into the city to get the things we discussed. If you are pregnant, we need to take care of your needs in accordance with that." He waited to get my agreement. "Okay, now that we're on the same page in that book, I will then spend my evening doing some heavy-duty math and preparing enough of this chemical to introduce into the local bodies of water. The zombies are already dying rapidly; we need them gone altogether."

I sighed with relief and looked at the clock. It was 3:17 p.m. in the afternoon. Jace wouldn't leave until nightfall. "I say we have sex," I told him.

He burst out laughing before taking me in his arms and giving me a big hug. He then took me by the hand and led me into the next room onto the double bed. I slowly took my clothing off, looking him square in the eye and smiling the entire time. His excitement grew more and more obvious. He tried to touch me numerous times, but I stopped him time and again.

Finally, he gently overpowered me, and lowering me to the bed he planted kisses all over my body. I moaned softly, over and over, as he got closer and closer to the spot I really wanted him to kiss, and when he arrived, kiss it he did. He brought me to climax again and again. I held the pillow over my face to keep from crying out, but I did not stop him.

Finally, it was my chance to return the favor, and I took him into my mouth hungrily. It didn't take long for his back to arch and his body to stiffen, and I took great pleasure in the fact that I had put him in this vulnerable state.

We lay spent on the mattress, both of us dozing in and out until finally, I was dreaming. I woke to his gentle shake and soft kisses. Oh, Jace...

"Get up, Leesh. We need to eat, and then I'm going into town. It's after seven." Upon hearing the time, I became fully awake. I put my feet on the floor and gathered my clothing together to dress. In no time I caught up to him in the kitchen, where he was preheating the oven to bake one of several frozen pizzas which he had brought back from town a few days ago.

We were giddy like schoolkids while we ate, sitting next to each other and holding hands while we chewed. The end was in sight, I just knew it. There was no need to fear that this house would be our final resting place. We had done the right thing, taken the right steps each and every time a step was called for, and finally it was paying off. We were going to see the end of this mess, and we were going to see it soon.

I disposed of our paper plates, a resource we had begun to use to save on our water supply. Jace packed some things into a backpack and made a list of what he wanted to get while in the city. Before letting him out the back door, he gave me a passionate kiss, one that gave of his entire being. I responded in kind. He then grabbed his bat, propped it on his shoulder, and smiled at me.

"I'll be back soon. Lock up and barricade, babe."

I smiled back. "You've got it. Hurry home." I then let him out and locked and covered the door.

Soon we would be free.

CHAPTER 18

Jace had left, and I decided that I would try to flip through the television channels. Maybe I could find something that was pre-taped and put on the air to appease the public. It was my honest hope that CNN would be broadcasting an update regarding the state of the 'zombie affairs.' I didn't let my hopes get too high, however. I figured most everyone was dead or wandering around close to it.

I flipped through the channels one at a time, each displaying an 'off the air' message. A couple of the nationwide networks were running loops of reruns; how they had the forethought to set that up, I will never know. When I arrived at CNN the same newsman was sitting at a desk, his skin pale and his eyes sporting matching luggage.

"From Tulsa, Oklahoma, breaking news... existing federal authorities have reported to the CNN newsroom that there are no survivors in the area... we repeat... Tulsa has no known survivors in the worldwide crisis which is currently taking place. John Thomas takes us live to the scene to discuss the outlook in that city."

I had stiffened up entirely before the newscaster had

even made his way through the first sentence. As soon as I heard Tulsa, I froze. This is what I had been waiting to hear, and now what I heard was heartbreaking. They, so far, had found no one alive in the entire area? Couldn't people be holed up in their homes?

The fact of the matter was that no one saw this coming. How could my parents have known, just getting off a plane from their vacation? There was no way. In seconds I considered my dad and mom. I was pregnant. I so badly wanted my mother to be alive, to run to Tulsa and to fetch her, to have her guidance and her help. This was nothing but a pipe dream. I knew this now.

My mind was filled with memories all at once. At the park with my mom as a small child. My father swinging me in large circles by my arms until I thought I would either die laughing or puke. The way my parents comforted me and made me laugh, caring for me fully the time I broke my arm in gymnastics, or any time I was sick or hurting. I jerked my mind from the memories to stop the tears from falling down my face. I wanted to scream, but I was afraid to do that. Instead, I buried my face in a throw pillow I held in my lap and sobbed until there were no more tears to be cried.

The news continued with its horrid relay, elaborating on the grim situation in my hometown. They showed newsreels of the area; the streets were filled with nothing but shuffling dead people. I thought of the life that might be growing inside me, and I had to jump up and run to the bathroom. What little dinner I had left in my stomach was emptied into the toilet like so much waste. I began to cry again. I didn't know how to be a mother. I still cried for my own mother! I curled up on the floor and cried until I was virtually spent. I didn't know what to do or who to turn to. Aside from Jace, I had absolutely no one.

My heart was broken in my chest; I knew with certainty that my parents, and more than likely the rest of my family, were all gone. I pulled myself together and went back to the living room to face the truth, occasional sobs escaping from my lips. I sat in the chair and turned the set up a bit louder.

"As you can see by the scene behind me, no one except myself and my crew are normal in all of Tulsa. The CDC reports that, while they are steadily searching for answers and a solid solution to this epidemic, they have made very little progress to date. The changes which have taken place in people all over the world have continued to perpetuate, and many of these… zombies… have turned from violence on each other to violence on normal, healthy humans. Government officials highly recommend that you stay indoors at all costs, and if you are confronted by one of these sick individuals try to avoid any contact. If contact is inevitable the only way to escape harm and save yourself is by striking them about the head. Other reports state…" I could listen to no more. I turned the television off with the remote and broke down again.

By the time I had pulled myself together, I had
realized it was a little after ten. Where was Jace? I could
picture every horrible scenario under the sun and
wound up sitting on the floor by the front window so I
could peek out the blinds and search for his headlights.
We were so far from the city, or so it seemed, that I
didn't see any signs of life for the first twenty minutes
that I sat there. Suddenly there was obvious movement
at the tree by the driveway entrance. I stared hard,
wondering if I was seeing things. Nothing. I continued
to strain my eyes, to no avail and had begun to believe I
had fallen asleep slightly and that the movement was
nothing more than a bit of a dream. Suddenly I saw it
again, but this time the movement was followed by a
figure staggering from the trunk of the tree. Jace?

My heart began thumping hard as I struggled to
make the figure out in the darkness. How I wish
something were lighting the yard area! Just then the
moon hit the figure's head, and for a split second, I got
a clear view: a gray-face was lurching toward the house,
full of hunger and purpose.

Confusion overtook me for a moment. Why would
it come here? There were absolutely no lights on, and
the television was off. What was attracting its interest?
Could these things actually smell the living? The
thought was almost too much to bear. It stole any hope
of hiding safely from these lifeless creatures. What was
the zombie doing here of all places?

I let go of the blind and crouched lower against the

wall by the window, peeling my ears, trying to hear anything I could. It was only a minute or so before I could hear the gravelly grunts which came from his body because of the effort he had to put into walking. Shortly after the pounding and yelling began.

I was terrified. I crawled across the floor to the kitchen, where my bat stood by the back door. I wrapped my hand around the bat's grip and turned it right-side up, drawing it close to me. The barricade at the front door shook slightly with each slam of the monster's fists, and with each failed attempt to break the door in he got angrier and angrier, his screams becoming more and more enraged and loud. I began to shake and cry, my sobs stifled by my own left hand. I could taste bile rising in my throat, and I thought I would surely be sick right there on the spot.

Suddenly the lower left part of the living room window was struck… hard. Again, this time cracking the glass. This zombie was weak. He was very likely near the end of his rope, or the window would have been gone in one fell swoop. Now I bit my lips to hold the vomit in, which permitted me to take my bat in both hands. His groans and screams became increasingly louder as he recognized that the strikes he administered to the window were actually beginning to get the job done. If there were any other gray-faces nearby, they would surely hear him and join the party. Jace, where the heck are you?

Right then I saw the headlights of Miss Smythe's car turn into the drive, bouncing off the wall. The zombie's fist came through the crack, shattering the lower part of that particular window section. The hand groped in the darkness as the zombie sputtered loudly, frustrated that his meal was not within his reach.

I heard the car door shut and suddenly the hand disappeared from the broken window. I jumped up and, bat in hand made my way over. Jace was approaching the zombie with his bat ready to go. The sluggish monster lurched toward him, arms swinging with each step, loud, hungry grunts spewing from his decaying head. Just like a major league player, Jace took a powerful swing at the zombie's head, connecting with full force. Rather than a thud, a thick squish resonated from the zombie's body. He fell to his knees, but still clawed at the air in Jace's direction. With his eyes glued to the monster, Jace walked to his right side, took aim, and splattered him once and for all. He was batting a thousand, and he must've enjoyed it because he was smiling with satisfaction.

Jace put the bat on the ground and looked around. He then grabbed the gray-face by the feet and dragged him across the road. While I couldn't clearly see, it appeared that Jace put his body in the culvert alongside the road. He came back and fetched the thing's mangled skull, tossing it in with the body like he was making a free throw. He then pulled the car into the garage, and I went to the kitchen to move the china hutch and let him into the house.

As soon as the door was blocked again, Jace put the things in his arms down on the table and turned to me.

Seeing his eyes was all it took; I collapsed into his arms, gasping sobs emitted from me, and the tears I thought were long drained dry poured from my eyes. My entire body convulsed with emotion, and he held me tightly.

"It's okay, Leesh. He's gone. He's dead," Jace said with confidence. He thought I was crying about the zombie. While the stress of that situation may have caused more tears, the only thing on my mind was my family, or what used to be of them.

I looked up at him. "My mom and dad, Jace. All of Tulsa. The government said... said..." I broke down yet again, losing control over my ability to talk.

"There was news? You were able to get news?" I nodded as best I could, and Jace took my hand and led me to the living room. He put me in the rocker and sat on the floor next to me. He used the remote control to turn the T.V. on, and for the next twenty minutes, we listened to a few normal people fill us in on what was happening on the late, great planet Earth. Jace was silent and sober. I continued to cry, and could barely make myself look at the set. They pinpointed nearly every major American city as having fallen victim to the infection which was overcoming mankind.

Finally, Jace turned the T.V. off, and the two of us sat still in the dark, turning the news over in our heads, struggling to accept what was happening. Finally he spoke.

"It seems they have no idea it's the water. Why didn't they mention the water? Could the CDC be keeping it a secret, and if so, why?" I just looked at him with wide eyes and shook my head. "It's okay, Alicia. We know, and we are going to do something about it."

In a split second my life with my mom and dad passed before my eyes, and I became even more determined to destroy the nastiness that was taking place all around us as soon as possible. I looked at Jace and nodded, smiling through my tears.

CHAPTER 19

Only minutes later we were in the kitchen, and Jace was unpacking the things he had brought. While he laid stuff on the table, he paid little attention to any of it. A bottle of iron pills, a few notebooks of paper, a pack of pencils, a calculator, multi-vitamins. He then pulled out the small box that contained the home pregnancy test. I already knew, but I think he wanted the peace of mind of knowing for sure, so without a word, I took the box from him and went into the bathroom.

Sitting on the side of the bathtub my thoughts had gone completely haywire. Pregnant? How could this be? Well, come on, Alicia, you have been having sex right and left for months with no protection whatsoever. Did you think you were immune to pregnancy? I simply shook my head in response to myself and stood up, pulling down my sweats as I did. I squatted over the toilet and began to pee, holding the stick in my urine stream just as the instructions directed. I then set it on the edge of the sink, not allowing the end to come into contact with the porcelain, and I wiped and pulled up my pants.

I opened the bathroom door and walked into our

lab, fetching the timer from the card table. I set it for ten minutes and headed back to the bathroom. Jace appeared.

"Well?" His eyes were bright, almost excited.

"It's going to take ten minutes for the results, Jace."

He let out a gust of air and nodded. He turned and went back into the kitchen to tend to whatever it was he was doing. I entered the bathroom and locked myself in. Taking a seat on the closed toilet lid I began to think about my parents again, and once more I found myself on the floor of the bathroom, crying my eyes out, my face buried in a towel so Jace wouldn't hear me. How I wish my mom was here doing this with me! She and my father would be a bit disappointed, but the joy they would feel at the thought of a new family member would outweigh the disappointment. They had been so easygoing, so down to earth... such wonderful parents. Why them and not me?

∞

The timer went off and jerked me back to reality. I turned it off and wiped my eyes, looking up at the stick on the sink. "Come on, Alicia. It's time for the verdict." I got up off the floor and picked up the stick.

It revealed a clear plus sign. Positive. Pregnant.

"Alicia?" Jace was already at the bathroom door. He must have heard the timer. I could tell he was anxious by the sound of his voice. I have to admit that I was a bit excited myself, no matter how much a pregnancy didn't make sense right now. The thought of something to actually be happy about was an idea I really needed.

I reached out and unlocked the bathroom door. The knob turned, and the door slowly opened. Jace looked at me with wide eyes.

"Well? What does it say?" He looked almost scared.

I kept my face devoid of emotion on purpose. Might as well keep him in suspense. Might as well make this moment as joyful and fulfilling as possible, regardless of the circumstances.

I held the stick out to him. "Why don't you see for yourself, Dad?"

He barely cast a glance over the little tattletale device before a huge "Whoop!" flew from his mouth. He picked me up and spun me around, before I knew it I was being smothered in his kisses. "Oh, Alicia. We have a reason bigger than us now. We have something that is part of you and me, and we will love it and do whatever it takes to protect it. Did you eat? Are you hungry? How do you feel? Are you okay? I didn't hurt you or make you…"

"Jace, I'm fine! I feel fine! Aside from a broken heart over my parents, I feel like a million dollars right now. Maybe this is just what we both needed to keep going. Maybe you are right." He took me by the hand and led me to the kitchen where he sat me down and put two pills, iron and a vitamin, in front of me.

"Take these and listen while we go over my math and my plan." I did as he told me and then focused on him completely.

He sat in the chair across the table. "Okay. I did a

bit of research on the laptop and found out how much water we are actually going to try to clean up in this city. We have the L.A. River, which is a dump anyway; that's going to be the toughest part. Then we have lakes and reservoirs, and it is only a small portion of that which we are going to be dealing with. Now, the problem is the ocean waters, but I don't think we should mess with Santa Monica Bay or the Dominguez Channel. I think we will be able to get pertinent results if we stick to the lakes and reservoirs. We will do the lakes first. I don't think those were initially polluted because the sewers which transport pharmaceutical waste do not empty into them. Regardless, we are talking about millions of gallons of water flowing out of the city per day. I have decided I am going to concoct forty gallons of the mixture. We will dump thirty gallons directly into the lake water, but we will test it first. We will hide out and take samples periodically to check the bacteria level, and if the results are good, we will head to the reservoir, for testing and treatment. If we don't like what we see, we will add more chemicals to the lake right away to avoid bacteria regrowth, and of course, we will have to take our equipment. I am also going to mix up some extra gallons, which will enable us to dump in extra gallons if we do not see the results we desire, but I believe we will, Alicia." His eyes were lit up with eagerness.

"Even if this doesn't work on the grand scale we hope, it will certainly cause enough damage to the bacteria to wipe out most, if not all, of the zombies milling around the area. That will make the remaining numbers easy to handle if there are any." He nodded in response, and then picked it up from there.

"The good news for us is that it hasn't rained. That will keep it from spreading while we contain it. The water from storms is not treated at all. Since we dumped the supply at the treatment plant all we need to focus on is the local bodies," he stated. "This is going to work. If nothing else it is going to give us a chance to get out of here safely and get in touch with the CDC with the information we have."

It was a good, solid plan, worthy of execution. I was anxious to get started. "When do you plan on getting the chemicals and the antibiotic?"

He looked at me and smiled. "I have a trunk full. I think it will be close to enough. I will begin whipping it up, and whatever else I need I can get in town. Right now I also have the back seat and passenger side of the sedan pretty much filled with empty milk jugs and bleach bottles. Those will hold the antidote. That was what took me so long; I was stopping and gathering… digging in the garbage. Is the still full? We need to use the water to clean the jugs out, and we need to get more water purified. We need a total of fifty gallons worth. One gallon per jug to wash and rinse, no more."

Everything was really falling into place, and I knew deep in my heart that it was going to work. We were going to be fine. Our baby was going to be fine. I stood up.

"Okay, Jace. Let's not put this off another minute. It's time to get started." I headed to the still, and Jace headed to the garage to begin bringing in empty bottles and other supplies. It was the beginning of the end.

CHAPTER 20

For the rest of the night and into the following evening Jace and I worked cleaning containers and mixing chemicals to refill them with. I napped on three occasions for only an hour at a time. I didn't want to leave all the work to him, not to mention the fact that the faster we completed the job the sooner we could put the meat of our plan into action. I wanted to get out of this house, but I wanted to be safe. I wanted the world I once knew to exist again, so even though Jace nagged me to rest and eat, I drove myself to help as much as possible.

Our spirits had lifted significantly, and the task was actually fun. We talked and laughed. I cried a couple of times, but only when my focus shifted to my parents. Jace would console me, and once I was calm, I would shake him off so we could get back to work. He was so patient and wonderful. Would I have ever met him had this terrible thing not happened? I knew I likely would not have, at least, not in this way or for this reason. I suppose if we were 'meant to be' nothing could have stopped our fated union, but who knew?

Jace had to go toward the city at around eleven the next morning to gather more containers. He was gone about an hour and a half. It was uneventful time; I continued to prepare chemicals so they would be ready when he returned. He came back with more jugs and bottles than we really needed, and once they were clean and filled with the antidote, we began to neatly pack them into the trunk and backseat of the sedan. They all fit neatly inside.

Next, we packed up our needed lab gear and notebooks, and once we were sure we had everything we needed, including some food for the trip, it was five o'clock in the afternoon. Jace wanted to leave at 8:30 p.m. and it sounded perfect to me. We grabbed a bite to eat, cold sandwiches and chips and lay down to catch a bit of sleep before it was time to leave. We were way too tired to think about making love, and my stomach had been pretty upset for the last few hours. The food had helped, but I was queasy lying next to him. He snuggled me close, and in minutes we were both dreaming.

∞

I woke to Jace gently nudging me awake. "Time to get the cobwebs out, Leesh." He was rubbing my back a bit, making me moan with contentment. It was times like this when I really wanted all of this to be nothing but a bad, bad dream, but alas…

We sat at the table having a couple of cups of instant coffee made with distilled water. Jace made sure our tank was full, so we would have water when we returned, while the zombies were dying off. While we drank, Jace spoke up about the baby.

"Alicia, I hope you feel good about the kiddo. I do. I'm excited, and I want us to both be happy." The look on his face was an almost childlike expectation, and it brought a smile to my face.

"I have to admit, before finding out about the condition of Tulsa I was a bit nervous. All I could think about was bringing a child into this disaster and trying to protect it and provide for it. Once I learned about my parents, well, my heart was broken even more. I realized that I was happy about it, and I couldn't share my joy with them... ever." I looked down at my hands and then back at him, smiling with reassurance. "I'm good, Jace. No worries."

He got a serious look on his face. "If and when we get through cleaning up this mess I want to marry you, Alicia. Would you marry me?"

I honestly hadn't thought about that aspect of it, and when I considered it, I had to admit that it made no sense to me. Marriage was a legal commitment. Was there even going to be 'law' anymore? Would a piece of paper matter?

"I don't know if it will matter, legally speaking, Jace. But if you want we can always take vows ourselves if it doesn't." His entire face began to shine as he smiled.

"You bet your ass." He drained his cup, prompting me to do the same. We stood and put our jackets on, then proceeded to move the china hutch, grab our sturdy bats, and head out to the car.

It was time to eradicate the gray-faces. I couldn't have been more excited.

We had decided to start with the lake. It was terribly polluted and had been for a while, and since the creek was fed by it, we might discover we don't need as much of the antidote, if any when it came time to do the reservoir. We drove to an area which provided us with a bridge under which we could set up shop, and we were even able to park the sedan discreetly. It was perfect for our mission.

We unloaded our equipment and set that up first, along with a small, battery-powered lantern he had brought from the garage at the house. We then began to unload thirty containers of the antibiotic mixture. Next, Jace filled a clean water bottle with water from the stinking lake and brought it to our little outdoor lab, where he immediately tested it.

"Take a look," he said to me, moving to give me access to the microscope. The water was filled with the vile bacteria. It had overtaken the drug molecules in the water to the point that they were hardly distinguishable at all. My stomach lurched hard. Between the look of the water and the smell of it, my delicate stomach was a mess. I jumped back, turned my head, and promptly deposited my sandwich and chips onto the rocks under the bridge.

Jace was right there, though, stroking my back and making soothing sounds. When I was done, he handed me a paper towel soaked in distilled water, and I cleaned my face off. He then gave me a drink so I could rinse out my mouth. I loved him; he was so very good to me.

When I had my wits about me, we conferred. "Okay, gross as it is, this is what we needed to see. Now it's time to get pouring." We had the bottles with the antidote lined up along the waterline so dumping would be fast. We took all the lids off. I listened closely to the sounds around me while we unscrewed the caps from the bottles. I could have sworn I heard the uneven shuffling sound of the feet of a gray-face, but at that point, one gray-face didn't matter. We could end him with one swing, so I didn't let myself become distracted.

When all the bottles were open, Jace said, "You start at this end. I'll start down here. Let's go." We began emptying the bottles into the lake at a record pace, and in less than two minutes the job was done.

Jace set the timer on his cell, and rather than have the alarm go off he simply watched the screen. We waited five minutes instead of only two, just for good measure, and when the time was up, he took a clean water bottle to the lake's edge and filled it. After bringing it back, he then placed two or three drops on a clean slide and put it under the scope. Waiting for him to look at the sample and give me a response was probably the most anxious period I had endured all day.

He looked up at me with a broad smile. Even in the shadows his eyes lit up and danced. "It's working, Alicia! It's working like crazy." I jumped over to the microscope and took a gander for myself. Sure enough, there was only a small amount of bacteria, and it was fading fast. The water almost looked as good as our distilled stuff.

I couldn't believe it. I stood up, but within seconds Jace had me in his arms hugging me tightly. "It's gonna be all right. I knew it! It's really gonna be all right."

I felt ecstatic but apprehensive. "Jace, we need to wait and test it again in a bit, you know, just to be sure."

"I know, I know, but it will be fine. Let's sit and wait another ten minutes or so." We planted ourselves on a blanket we had brought. I used distilled water and rubbing alcohol to clean up our slides and droppers while we waited, drying them thoroughly when they were clean.

After another ten minutes had passed Jace filled another empty bottle and brought it up for testing. I was a bit doubtful; how could it go so smoothly? No one had been able to clean this water, ever. Now we were going to do it in an hour's time?

The water passed the test with flying colors at that.

We were both so excited and anxious to get to the creek, which was a fairly good distance from here. We started to pack our things into the car, and that was when we heard the shuffling, louder than before, and directly over our heads. We scooted up the hill which led beneath the bridge. A zombie was going down the same hill on the other side of the bridge. He wanted to get to the water. He needed a drink.

We both looked around and seeing that it was all clear we shoved the rest of our things into the sedan as quickly as possible. We then got into the car, rolled up the windows, and made sure the doors were securely locked. We watched. Within seconds the gray-face jerked his way into view, and tripping on a rock or something, he lost his footing and fell the rest of the way down the hill. It took all I had not to crack up laughing, so I put my hand tightly over my mouth and kept my eyes on the scene playing out before me.

Once he regained what was left of his composure, he crawled on his hands and knees to the water's edge, where he proceeded to completely submerge his entire head into the now-clean H2O. Suddenly he jerked his head violently out of the water and screamed. It was angry, horrifying, and bloodcurdling. How, I didn't know, but that monster could tell that the water was not the same.

Again he put his head in. He pulled it out and smelled the water. Screaming again he stood and began to have what I would call a violent tantrum right on the banks of the lake. Suddenly from the road zombies began to come down to the banks of the lake. They were all either screaming or groaning. They headed to the lake and smelled, tasted, and touched the water. Then they all proceeded to go completely off the deep end.

Jace must've sensed that it was time to go. He started the car, which got their attention immediately. Man, were they ever pissed. They all started toward us, arms flailing, and vile sounds coming from their throats. Every motion was full of anger and intent, even though they all lacked the coordination or power to get to us quickly. You could see that they either sensed or smelled our blood.

Even as they made their way to the car, they began to drop off. There had to be more than fifteen of them, but they lost three on their way. One must have been closer than we thought. She started hitting the trunk and back window with all she had, working her way up my side of the car. Her screams were filled with furious desperation.

"Jace, go! What the heck are we waiting for?" He put the sedan into gear and floored the gas pedal, steering erratically. We jerked our way up the hill, zombies struggling to keep up. One had a hold of the bumper, and we dragged him halfway up before losing him on the rocks and grass. Then we were on the road, Jace speeding away from the lake. Gray-faces were staggering up both sides of the road, heading to try to get their fix for the night. It was easy to assume this was a regular nightly ritual. Otherwise, why would there be so many all at once? Hundreds were making their way to the water's edge. They would head toward the car, hitting it as we passed. If they got in the way, Jace hit them without a second thought, their dusty bodies breaking apart like so much tissue paper-covered bone.

Finally, after what seemed like miles, we took a right, and the zombie parade seemed to end. I sat back in my seat and took a breath. "Nice moves, Jace."

His eyes flitted from the road to the rearview mirror and back again. "Thanks, sexy. Now that takes care of Baloa Lake. We were halfway done."

CHAPTER 21

When we reached the reservoir, which I had never visited, I could see what Jace meant when he stated that we had only a small portion of the actual reservoir to deal with. It was nothing like I expected, and there was really no thought that we were going to run into any gray-faces during this visit. By now it was around one in the morning, and all was completely still and silent all around the area where we were. Jace even left the headlights to the car on, aiming them at the spot where we were to set up our little portable lab.

We got our equipment out and set up, waiting to unload bottles of the antidote until we were sure how much we would need. We went through the same process. Jace collected water from the reservoir and put it on a clean slide, then took a good look.

"Alicia, check this out," was all he had to say.

I looked through the microscope and was surprised at how little of the bacteria was present in the water. "It's not going to take nearly what we thought, Jace."

He nodded. "I know, and that's a good thing, but we are gonna dump ten in anyway. It certainly can't hurt." We proceeded to soldier back and forth to and from the car with the ten jugs of antidote, and this time we were a bit more lax in our administration methods, uncapping and dumping them into the reservoir one at a time. After our fifteen minute wait, we conducted another test, and the water was virtually spotless.

"Okay, we'll wait ten more minutes and take a final sample. We have ten bottles left. I want to drive back to the creek, but this time we are going to get a sample from further up the creek. We'll drive along the creek and stop and dump the last ten in one at a time as we go. It will be more dispersed that way."

I nodded in agreement. "Good thinking."

The second sample came back just as pretty as the first, so we went about packing up our gear and making our way back to the creek. We stopped at the creek's side six times between Baloa Lake and the reservoir. Along the way, we counted over sixty zombies lying lifeless in the road. I was in shock at the number. What was even more surprising was the lack of live zombies anywhere within sight. Had they all made it to their destination and was this why they were not out and about?

Every time we stopped, we would test the water. As we neared our original spot, it became progressively clearer, and each test showed bacteria being destroyed at a high rate. We would add a gallon, test again, and every time the results were stunning. Jace also took a bottle full from each stop to observe again once we were back at the house.

When we arrived at the bridge, Jace stopped the car

but left it running. There were no zombies in sight at all.

"Are we really coming back here Jace? Are you crazy?"

"Like a fox," he responded. He undid his seat belt and grabbed an empty bottle to get another sample from under the bridge. "Stay right here, and keep the doors locked until I come back. Do not get out of the car for any reason, Alicia."

He hopped out with his bottle and shut the door, which I locked behind him. He jogged toward the hill which led down under the bridge. In only a few minutes he came walking back to the car. That was a great sign.

After he got in and locked up I asked, "No gray-faces?"

"About thirty of them are lying down there completely out of commission. We'll check out the road they were walking on as we head home and see what the view is like."

∞

Now it was nearly five in the morning, and we could see very well. On the road home, we counted over one hundred and fifty of the dead-heads lying lifeless and still. This was the reason Lilith, my roommate, guzzled constantly. Without a consistent supply of the bacteria, the brain ceased to function and drive the body, and there were no internal organs to maintain life at all. They were virtually addicted to death.

Rather than head directly back to Miss Smythe's home, we drove through the city center. There was the random zombie here and there, some were in groups shuffling and bumping into each other, and others were trying to tear each other to bits with what little strength they had left. Neither Jace nor I caught sight of one real live, blood-pumping and heart-pounding human being during our drive. If any were out there, they were hiding pretty well.

I had my doubts that many were even left. Besides us, that is.

∞

Back at the house, we lined up our bottled samples: we had one from Baloa Lake and a total of seven taken from various spots along the creek and reservoir. Each was marked with the time and exact location, and Jace had a notebook in which he had jotted down initial test results and what time we administered the antidote at each location. It would make for a very thorough comparison.

Once we had the microscope ready and all of the slides and droppers clean again we began testing each sample. The results could not have been more pleasing: all of the samples came back wonderfully clean! We compared each to a sample of the distilled water. Perfect.

Next, we made our way to the living room where we sat and turned on CNN to catch the latest news. We both half-expected it to be off the air, but the same newscasters were on the air, looking frightened and exhausted. Even the reporters on location at various cities could do nothing to hide the bags under their eyes, and I doubted very highly that they even cared.

"While most of the major metropolitan areas and surrounding towns have experienced a major population wipe-out due to the appetites and anger of these terribly mutated zombies, military forces flying over the Los Angeles area have reported that the walking dead in the area are slowly but surely dying off. Here is Jill Montgomery with an update from the California coast, with information supplied directly from sources at the CDC as well as from military spokespersons. Here's Jill."

"Thank you. Los Angeles was only one of the world's major metropolitan areas to be virtually wiped out by the zombies, or mutated humans who have been running rampant for the last seven or eight months. While medical professionals at the Centers for Disease Control finally released information last night that they had pinpointed the issue to contaminated water, they have no idea what the source of the contamination is or was, and they are still battling to remedy the issue. As we reported earlier, if you are able to view and comprehend this broadcast it is essential that you do not ingest or bath in the water, if you have been able to at all. In the meantime, military forces assigned to the LA area have told us that the zombies occupying Los Angeles and the surrounding area are literally dropping off like flies. As you can see from this videotape, provided by the Air Force not an hour ago, there are literally piles of bodies lying around, and the number is consistently growing. The CDC has sent a crew into LA to test the water in the Los Angeles River to find out what exactly has taken place to turn the tide in sunny California. If anyone has any information, please contact the CDC immediately, or get in touch with local armed forces units as soon as possible. Phone numbers flashed on the screen. This is Jill Montgomery for CNN, reporting that bluer skies may be in our future."

Jace and I looked at each other for only a fraction of a second before he jumped up and went to the kitchen for my cell phone. He used it to input the number and then tapped the screen to direct the smartphone to dial for him. In no time we were on speakerphone relaying to the powers that be exactly what had taken place in our lives over the last several months, but especially over the last several days.

After a couple of hours and a promise that the military would be coming to take us to safety, we finally hung up. We were both wound up and excited. We were safe, and we were going to have a life after all.

I sat in the rocker with Jace on his knees before me. His head was on my tummy, and I ran my fingers through his hair. His breath was steady and even, and he seemed truly relaxed for the first time since I had met him. I wondered if I was the same in his eyes.

He looked up at me. "How do you feel?"

"Amazing," I replied. "And you?"

He smiled. "Outstanding. More alive and hopeful than I could have ever imagined. Are you hungry?"

"Hmmm. Let me think... for you."

Jace's smile grew wider, and he leaned forward to initiate an amazing, long-lasting kiss. Before I knew it, we were snuggled together on the floor, spent and half-asleep. Before my dreams overtook me, I heard him say in a heartfelt tone, "Alicia, we literally have the rest of our lives to do this. I love you so much."

"I love you, too. I really do."

We were both looking forward to forever.

ENTREATY

This book was made possible by reviews from readers like you. Reviews fuel my creativity. If you enjoyed this novel, I implore you to please write a review and share your experience on the retailer's website. The livelihood for authors is entirely dependent on reviews, and I must say, it is the largest obstacle as a struggling author that I have encountered. Please tell a friend, tell a loved one about this read. With your help, I will be one step closer to overcoming this obstacle. In return, I thank you from the bottom of my heart, and sincerely appreciate your time and effort.

Humbled, with gratitude,

R.W.K. Clark

ABOUT THE AUTHOR

I am a father of two beautiful children, Jon and Kim. They are my motivating forces; they are the lighthouse in this vast ocean. In my life, they are the air that I breathe; they are the oasis in this desert of uncertainty. They are my greatest joy in life and my number one priority. I have a long list of hobbies, and I attribute that to my lust for life! I like to surround myself with positive people, who share the same interests. Family values, the arts, outdoors, nature, and travel are tops on my list. I embrace attending cultural and artistic events because I believe dramatic self-expression is the window to the soul. I wear my heart on my sleeve, and I still believe in chivalry, and I always treat people the way I want to be treated.

www.rwkclark.com